Hiram Hoyt Richmond

Montezuma

An Epic on the Origin and Fate of the Aztec Nation

Hiram Hoyt Richmond

Montezuma
An Epic on the Origin and Fate of the Aztec Nation

ISBN/EAN: 9783743383463

Manufactured in Europe, USA, Canada, Australia, Japa

Cover: Foto ©Raphael Reischuk / pixelio.de

Manufactured and distributed by brebook publishing software (www.brebook.com)

Hiram Hoyt Richmond

Montezuma

MONTEZUMA.

AN EPIC

ON

THE ORIGIN AND FATE

OF THE

AZTEC NATION.

BY

HIRAM HOYT RICHMOND.

SAN FRANCISCO:
GOLDEN ERA CO
1885.

CONTENTS.

— ◆

EGYPT.

AZTLAN.

ANAHUAC.

ARGUMENT OF THE POEM.

From the moment of my earliest acquaintance with Colonial History, I have felt all the pressure of a task laid upon me, tightening its grasp as I reached maturer years ; that of an attempt to rescue the Aztecs from their letterless and mythical position in history, to the position which their possibilities at least argue for them ; and this feeling has been far less the outgrowth of the enthusiasm awakened for the Aztecs, as the indignation felt at the whole conduct of the Spanish Conquest.

Realizing the gravity of the task, I have been led to carefully weigh and investigate the different theories advanced as to the origin of the Aztecs, and to adopt the argument of the poem as the best ground on which to unite the Sun Worship of the East with the Mythology of of the West.

Reverently, and with a full realization of how great must ever be the distance between the actual work and the ideal of my early inspiration, I lay the gathered chaplet at the shrine of old Chapultepec, and only regret that the fruiting should have fallen so far short of the promise of its blooming.

To Hubert Howe Bancroft the living, and W. H. Pres-

cott the dead, differing as they do in some very material
respects, yet essentially the same in spirit, I wish to record my indebtedness for their admirable and exhaustive
works that have induced to a final effort the poem of
which this is prefatory.

Some years since, I found in an abridged history of
the United States, a brief outline that led me back to the
Dispersal at Shinar (certainly a safe location for a speculative beginning) for the origin of the Aztec race.

It occurs to me now, with a shade of the ludicrous,
that if safety were the all-important thing in the premises,
I might have gone back a step farther to the figs and
pomegranites of Eden, and prayed for the shade of Adam
to cover the exotic which I have humbly tried to rescue
from what seems to me to be an underserved obscu-
rity. The careful analogies drawn between Egypt and
the Aztecs by both Prescott and Bancroft could be better met by locating the origin at Shinar than at any other point, as it takes us back to a date where we may con-
sistently locate the Shepherd Kings and the overrunning
of Mizraim by them, a part of Egypt's early history which
is outlined (more or less briefly) by nearly all early histo-
rians

As to the initial period of Sun Worship and its origin,
I could of necessity have but little aid, and if I have
seemed a little too speculative, I have only this apology :
The prodigy of Egypt's prehistoric development, and the
manufacture of glass, antedating historic research.   It

needs no great imaginative tension to crown some incip-
ient philosopher not only with the discovery of glass,
but, that in its proper shape, it could be made to concen-
trate the solar rays, and produce fire ; and at that day and
age, what possible superstitions might result from these
discoveries !

After the re-establishment of the Mizraim descent, and
the consequent expulsion of the "Sons of Lud," the line
of their journey is the natural outgrowth of their religious fanaticism. They know that India and the far East
are inhabited, and they seek the uninhabited track for
their exit.

The Mound Builders seem to be historic cousins of the
Aztecs, certainly the superiors of the aborgines of the
North and Middle Atlantic.

The expulsion of the Mound Builders will admit of
many theories, and I have simply adopted the one that
occured to me as consistent with the Christian inspiration
of all great events.

The settlement of Mexico by the Aztecs, (as a branch
of the Mound Builders) follows naturally in the wake of
previous events, and the chain is thus made complete,
with no serious hazard to its consistency as merely speculative drama, leading up to what is plainly historical.

I have striven to be historically consistent, following
the letter of events closely, taking conjectural ground in
but few instances.

If I have seemed to be censorious, even to rancor at

times, I have only given vent to the repressed indignation of Prescott and other authors on the subject of the Spanish Conquest.

The only possible justification for the excesses of Cortez and his adherents, is the age in which the Conquest took place ; and those who seek to justify it in this way, point to the opening of the present century, and to Napoleon, decoying the imbecile king and the weak Asturias into abdication and banishment to make room for his brother Joseph. This is a plague-mark upon the present century, and though a plain case of retributive justice through the visiting of the sins of the fathers upon the children, still the fact remains that the attempt to bring *right* of any multiple of wrongs, must always record a failure.

A sufficient answer to the latitude of the age, is the fact that a corresponding age gave us Plymouth, and not long after Penn's colony ; nor can the Spaniards claim the same justification for excesses as these coincident colonists, all of whom had felt the lash of religious intolerance. The Spanish Conquest, antedating the divisions that followed the reformation, has no such covert for their lustful excrescences.

Any system of religious ethics that severs human responsibility from the domain of conscience, and furnishes a market for the indulgences that cover all the excesses of the body politic, cannot be expected to bring forth the best of fruit from a bloom so blighted by human lust, and so blackened by human selfishness.

If, amid all of their intolerence and deceit, they had respected the homely records and the grotesque land-marks of the nation they destroyed, the cavaliers might have shown them as a slight palliation,and at once furnished the historian the shadow of justification for their abuses ; but the mental caste that could adopt any, and every de-vice of deception and treachery to accomplish its ends, threw itself at once into the arms of a priestcraft, if pos-sible more implacable than themselves ; and obedient to their demands, tore down their landmarks, and ground their records to powder.

Surely, there is no fanaticism like religious fanaticism, and no licentiousness like that of the unbridled devotee of the Church.

Finally, as a whole, I feel confident that my effort will not fail to create food for thought , and eventually justify the effort which called it forth. To a nature partially Huguenot in its origin, and more so in sympathy and in-clination, I have tried to add the temperate element that would impart freedom from undue prejudice and passion; but as the work is of necessity vindicatory on the one hand, and repressive on the other, I have been com-pelled to use good, plain Saxon words in the closing pages, justified only by the verity of their signification.

The body of the work is given in decimeters, varying

in only a few cases where the expression seemed to require a different form.

I would rather not close these already extended remarks without recording my testimony, with that of others, of the positive pleasure experienced both in the progress and completion of a work of this character; and if I shall have been as fortunate in securing and retaining an auditory, I shall be twice blessed ; for our highest ambition should ever be that of contributing to the happiness of others.

The reward of earnest labor, conscientiously performed, is the prize only *once* exceeded in the economy of things, and that *once* beyond the ken of our divulgence ; yet, may we not hope that there is no actual severance between the earthly type and the heavenly reality, that the crown honestly won, and the prize worthily gained on earth, may both, retaining their semblance, the more perfectly glow in the clearer atmosphere of heaven.

H. H. R.

MONTEZUMA.

PART FIRST.

EGYPT.

THE DISPERSAL AT SHINAR.

As mariner upon the rocky sea,
  Without a compass, helm, or heavenly hope,
A part of Earth's great ancestry to be
  Upon the plains of Shinar; and they grope
In nature's darkness; they have lost the way
  That leadeth to the Father, and can find
No clue of that great Presence, once their stay,
  And still as near ; but sin doth make us blind,
And when it fastens on the soul, the Father fades away.

How wholly lost, when man cannot descry
  One token of his Maker in the soul—
One step remains, the animal must die ;
  But death has superseded its control,
Since the immortal "Ego" is no more,
  The spirit gone from its companion, dust—
The ashes are but animate in vain
  When love, and light, have given place to lust
And conscience gives no puncture for its pain.

Thus were they gathered, in this day far gone,
  So near the causeway of the almighty past,
That retrospect brings close, the thought of God—
  We wonder that a cloud could overcast,
So primitive a people, that the Shepherd's voice
Should leave no lingering echo, for the ear, so tokened
    and so choice.

And they would build a city, and a tower
  Whose top would reach the very verge of Heaven; —
The puniest arm, is puissent in power,
  When to its grasp supernal aid is given ;
But muscles may, like cordage, swell the arm,
  And arteries, like rills of mountains flow.
Weak is the blood that breakers them to harm, —
  The fires of passion but a moment glow.

They, as the infants play upon the rim
  Of ancient Ocean, had been rocked to sleep
In the bare arms of Nature ; she would trim
  Her lamps for them, and patient vigil keep
Upon their slumbers; and Heaven, to them,
  Was but a brilliant, close-spread canopy,
Or crystal dome, a sort of diadem
  Just out of easy reach, and they could see
No reason why they might not build a tower
  Would intercept it; and their foolish pride
Supposed this little caprice of the hour,
    Through all the after age, would witness of their power.

They made them bricks, and steadily they reared
   The spiral column heavenward ; the Great Eye
Bent vigilantly on them, as they neared
   The upper ether, silent as the sky
Draws round its garniture ; into each soul
   Crept the first rootlets of an unknown tongue;
Each household head placed under his control
   The elements of intercourse, first flung
Together by the great Teacher ; just before
   When they had dropped from their exulting hands
The rough-made tools ; they closed forevermore
   Their mutual labor, though in other lands
They could resume their use, this was the last
   Of the poor monument that they had reared—
The workmen stand in wonderment aghast,
   Though they had wrought together, and had cheered
Each other in their task, each quivering lip
   Breathed but confusion to the other's ears,
No more from common cup of thought they sip,
   But forced to strangerhood for many, many years.

In what a school was fashioned our first thought.
   How the poor soul is dumbed, and quivering,
When we conceive what the Great Master wrought.
   How are we littled, what a nameless thing
"Is man, that thou art mindful" thus "of him."
   Thou settest up, and pullest down, and we—
Our hearts are hushed, our vision is made dim—
   Mites in the balance of imponderate destiny.

A camp in Central India, 'neath the palms,
    And where the lap of nature is so full,
That all the world may beggar it of alms
    And drink of its repletion ; a mere tool
Of hungry Kingdoms, thirsty Dynasties —
    The finger-tips of Alexander's arm—
The plethorite of the Augustan age—
    The gilt that margins all the tapestries
Down through middle ages; and the charm
    That lends a mellow fragrance to the page
Of her, the Island Queen, whose arm meets arm
In the embrace of earth, her borders refuge from avenging
        harm.

A journey into Egypt, with their flocks before,
And peaceful conquests back, an opening door
    To vast historic truths, a Niobe
Moaning her children's travail in advance,
    A restless nomad people, like the sea,
Stirred by involuntary force, whose billows dance
To music of the spheres, stern Autocrat, and yet a slave
        to its own mastery.

SOJOURN IN EGYPT.

O Egypt ! how shall we approach thy face ?
How steal from thy dumb lips one scrap of song ?
    Thou stand'st alone, and sendest from thy place
One word, that human lips have shaped for thee,
To seal thy mighty arch with " mystery."

Time calls his children 'round him, and they each
Give answer to their names; gray Troy and Greece
  Pour out the lesson their dumb lips would teach,
Carthage, Phœnicia, Parthia and Rome
  Clothe death with all the eloquence of speech ;
And each form linklets of an unbroke chain.
  But they are youthful; in perspective dim
As if unmoved with either joy or pain.
  With arms enfolded, and with eye all fixed,
A silent portal in the track of time.
  In the rough surge of nations still unmixed,
Where the great fathers left thee in the Sphinx,
  And heaped the sands upon thy broken links,
Thou dost look down the ages to defy
Tradition, inspiration, and all future progeny.

She sleeps as they advance; their lowing kine
  And noisy herds before them, and with the flute
And siren song, they win, as with old wine,
  Their way into the slumbering and the mute
Endormir of old Nile ; but Egypt wakes,
  And breast to breast, opposes their advance.
In vain against the shepherd crew, she breaks
  Her ill-spent arrows, shattered every lance,
And Mizraim's sons the rod of empire yield
  To sons of Lud; they spread their many tents
On Nile's unequaled garniture of field,
  The one discordant note in her great eloquence.

How Nature heals what man has thus laid waste,
   The stoic songsters of the worlds orchaste
Sing the same song, for friend and foe alike,
   They lift no arm upon a world defaced
With war's stern tread, but with one voice they strike
   The note of conquest or the requiem
Of some o'ertoppled Realm, Nature moves on
   To shame the bugle blare, or sound of drum,
And sets her thousand nestlings in the dust of the
      unnumbered nations that are gone.

One after one, in stately march of time,
   Kings pass, like common people, to the dust ;
Unless by over-reaching, and the crime
   Of too much selfhood, they are rudely thrust
A little sooner to their Maker's hands,
   And their succession made accelerate
By that potention, which each scepter mans,
   To fix each calendar, with human date.
No mortal is a law unto himself,
   And much less, he who holds the reins of power;
For wisdom seldom is concentrated so,
   That one weak soul is master of the hour,
Unquestioned arbiter of human fate,
   Free to subdue, to persecute, to kill
The soul that reaches this enlarged estate,
   Meets with a giant in the human will,
That soon or late, will crush him with its skill.

SUN WORSHIP.

Dread Guard! whose portal is another world,
  Thy mandate never can be circumscribed;
Only that Hand thy car to being whirled,
  And set thy lips, forevermore unbribed,
Can break the seal of silence; we look out,
  And over both eternities, and waste
Our energies, to find some well-tried route
  Out of life's labyrinth, where we may taste
The true nepenthe that disarms all doubt.

Beyond all human ken the key is kept;
  Our prison is too strong, and will not break,
Our Keeper's eyes are those that never slept,
  Yet never slept for love and our dear sake;
Touched by God's hand, the bolts will always yield;
  We rule him; in our weakness, if we ask,
Our asking turns the desert to a field,
  And shapes a coronal of every task.
A pestilence has struck this favored land—
Religion pleads in health; it now must take command.
The gods of Egypt, all are impotent,
  The people beat the empty air in vain;
No orgie gains the purchase of content, ·
  Their altars only mock the nation's pain.
The King has called a council to discuss
  The best-laid methods of religious thought.
Of counselors, there is an overplus,

And many are the schemes that they have brought,
All conjured since they lost their way.   The years
   Had slowly passed, since God himself had spoke,
And hearts are human things, and their hot tears,
   Melting their souls to harmony, in echoing murmur
      broke:

      O Soul! that is all song,
        O Heart! that is all love,
      O Right! that knows no wrong,
      O Arm! that is all strong,
        Upon our bosoms move.

      O Eye! that is all sight,
        O Voice! that is all sound,
      O Life! that is all might,
      O Wing! that is all flight,
        Where, where can you be found?

      O Ear! that only hears,
        O Voice! that only sings,
      O Eye! that knows no tears,
      O Time! that counts no years,
        Lend us thy gift of wings.

      O Faith! that wants no form,
        O Hope! all unafraid,
      O Sun! without a storm,
      O Summer! always warm,
        Where shall our hearts be stayed?

O Spirit! infinite,
O thou unchanging Word!
Whose echoes round us flit,
With all the past enlit,
O make thee to be heard!

So sang the gathered choral of the King,
And so, with saddened hearts, responded all
The gathered multitude; with what a spring
Is set the chords of Nature; and the call
From any searching soul a unit is
Of universal and insatiate thirst.
The longing story one may sing as his,
Responsive hearts all echo with the first,
Which shows how deep are all of our desires;
How earnestly we peer out in the dark!
How are we freighted, all, with latent fires!
How, on our souls and in our hearts, the Master
leaves His mark!

There rose, from on the outskirts of the crowd,
One bowed with lengthened years, yet nobly bent
With the more potent weight of earnest thought;
His massive brain and princely bearing lent
A more than common strength to his clear eye,
As, on his shepherd's staff, his form was bent;
Near to the King, with faltering step he came,
And spake, as if a master spake, with all his soul
aflame.

"Oh King, and sons of Lud! No pardon asks
Old Kohen for the words that leap his lips;
No earthly throne gives warrant to my voice;
But he, the God, of whom our fathers told,
The God of Noah; he, at whose command
The patriarch bent to labor; and till twice
A hundred harvest moons had waned, wrought on
The ark, and saved the seed of man to earth,
He, he, has spoken! and his words have sunk
So deeply in my heart I must be heard.—

'Thus saith the Lord: 'O truant sons of Lud,
Why grope ye in the dark, why not return
To the great Father's house?   How have I called
And waited for an answer to my suit!
O sons of men, return! repent! believe!
Where have ye wandered, that ye have not heard
The voice of your Jehovah in the wind,
And on the storm and tempest, when in wrath
He thunders in the ears of men; repent!
And on the desert in the hot simoom
Writ fervent words to warn you of your way.

''I am the God, of whom your fathers spake;
Out of all chaos did I call the earth,
And out of dust, your great ancestor made;
And hardly his clay swaddlings put on,
Ere from his rib I called his helpmeet forth,

"'Your mother Eve; I have bespoken wrath;
Yet, on the threshold of your life I placed
The ministry of love, and with my lips
   Kissed the clay to life.   How have I longed
To hold the race as I their fathers held,
Encircled in the Everlasting Arms;
But ye would not; ye are yourselves, a law,
To your own beings in my image made,
And ye must choose to live, to love, to learn.
How great is my compassion, and how long
I have kept watch, and waited for my lost!

"'My very anger is the throne of love.—
Because I could not lose the multitudes,
The myriads of millions yet unborn,
I spoke your father Noah into work,
And set afloat the remnant of his loins,
And oped the gates of Heaven to flood the earth.
I saw the race go down to watery graves,
In sorrow; and I saw a deeper wound
Had I but spared; I struck the seedling off,
Rather than smite the tree; I move in storms
To purify; and in the tempest smite
Only to save.
               I saw the impious hands
Your fathers raised in Shinar, and I came
And in the night, gave each another tongue,
And scattered their device, and smote their lips

That they raised not to mine. How could I see
Their folly and not smite?   I loved them so;
Ye, who have children, look within your hearts,
And in them see the miniatures of mine;
More of the parent than your soul can feel.

" ' Behold in me the source and spring of love;
I followed with paternal care to Ind,
I saw, and I stood guard upon your steps;
More than a father's love was in my soul,
More than a mother's tenderness inurned.
The mountains are the mole-hills of my strength;
Yet am I weak in love; I would not send
One single child to the eternal world
All unprepared; but ye have gone astray;
Ye are my flock, and I would turn you back
Before the wolves shall fatten of your flesh.

" ' Bring offerings from your herds, the choicest bring,
(Are they not also mine?) and altars build
And offer them thereon, but further bring
The contrite heart, and the unsullied hand,
Bring, as your fathers told you, Abel brought,
And I will meet you on the altar's brink,
With fire from Heaven, and consume it all.
Ask not again to look upon my face;
Ye cannot look, and live; I only speak,
As I now speak, through Kohen; he it is,
Out from among you I have set apart

" 'To be my sponsor; listen to my words:
Build up your altars, offer from your best;
Am I not better than the best you have?
When ye have builded, pray; pour out your hearts
As ye pour out the blood; prayer is the key
To my most inner soul; the voice of love
Is prayer.   It is the angel's wing that fell
Never yet short of Paradise.   The voice
That trembles on the lips of infancy,
When reaching out to reason, and the last
That passes with the shadow of the sun
When life's last slope is reached, and never yet
Has the repentant spirit left unalmsed.

" ' Have ye not heard how "Enoch walked with God,
And he was not," because I drew him up?
He kept so closely locked in my embrace,
That there was nothing left of him to die.
So would I have you walk, and learn the way;
For I am very near each human soul,
And ye may blend your being into mine,
And, losing self, be only found of me.
Ye all through Adam sinned; but there will come
A time when, in the second Adam, will the first
Transgression be atoned; your altars then
May all be turned to ashes; for I send
My best beloved, my ever blessed Son,
The Prince of Peace, to save the sin-cursed earth

" ' From the first great offense, and to prepare
The creature for creation's judgment day ;
Himself, upon the altar will be placed,
A final offering for the sins of men.

" 'Thus is our justice smothered o'er with love;
The law is satisfied, when Love, made King,
Bends down the neck to bear the ills of earth.
Therefore return:
And I will warm you back to perfect life,
If you but follow me.   Come in, and rest,
I am your husbandman, and all I have
Is on my table ; feast, and fill yourselves.
I am your vintner; here is wine, and here
Is honey ; satisfy your wants, I am
Your garden, Eden is restored in me.
    O children that are lost ! be found again ;
I am your Shepherd, and my arms shall bear
The weak ones of the flock.   Do any thirst?
I am your Spring, your parched lips to cool ;
Come and be one with me ! and I will be
More than your souls could ever frame to ask.
    Come to my open arms, O sons of men !
They are not full without you ; in my heart
Is loneliness, though from itself it draw
Companionship.   Had I but called to life
The pliant clay of Adam, and not breathed
My spirit in his nostrils, then could he

"'Filled out his measure with a lesser life,
Without the test of law; but how much more
To live as he could lived, divinely great
In mastery of earth, and only on
The single test, obedience to our will;
Yet, he fell short, and I foresaw it all
And suffered it, that human eyes might see
The glories of redemption, and behold
The one Incarnate Son, the Soul of Love,
The Second Self of Me.

"'O sons of men,
Fall down! behold his coming in a glass;
Behold and see him, in the fire I send
From Heaven upon your altars, and repent;
And when the time is fully ripe, behold
He cometh in the flesh! and ye shall see
The very Son and Sanction of my heart.
Oh! is it not enough? Can even I
Do more? Your children shall behold my words
Grown to fulfillment, and they all shall see
The Son of God become the Son of Man;
And ye may see, by faith, if ye implant
The tree of your redemption, so its leaves
May cover Egypt and the rest of earth.

"'The pestilence that darkens at your door
Came as a cry, from Mizraim in bonds;

" 'Strike off his chains! and I will lift you up.
Love ye your neighbor, as ye love yourselves;
His bruises and your pestilence shall pass
Together from the land. Live ye pure lives,
And all your blackness shall become as snow.
Make room for me among you; in the morn
Let rise your incense to the throne of grace;
Bring me your noon oblation; in your thanks
Let evening have its holicaust of love.
When spring puts forth her promise, offer up;
When summer comes, enladen with its growth,
And when the harvest moon, with ripened sheaves,
Measures the fullness of my great regard;
Yea! when the winter brings the time of rest,
Forget-me-not ! forget-me-not ! but pour
Into each crevice, of the well filled year,
The overflow of all your thankfulness.

" ' Come in the Spring and Summer of your lives,
And in the yellow leaves of Autumn come,
And in the snow and Winter of your age ;
Come any time, but come ! stay not away !
And I will give you rest ; and ye shall not
Go out again forever ; but shall shine
Bright as the brightest stars, and ye shall sing,
As never angels sang ; and every soul
Be swallowed up in sunshine evermore."

He ceased ; and there arose from out the crowd
The murmuring voice of question on the air;
Some thought him moved of God, and long and loud
Gave acclamation in his favor ; "Where,"
Cried they, "can such authority be found?
Whence come those gracious words, if not from God ?—
Power, wisdom, love, entripled in the sound
A mother's tenderness, a father's rod."

Then spake the unctious King ; and through the King,
The man; for he was but a tattered rag
Of royalty : "What is this wondrous thing,
Old Kohen, you propose? Make haste, let lag
Your purpose ; why is it, we cannot speak
Face unto face with your great Deity?—
Our fathers say old Noah did—what leak
Has sprung between us, that we cannot see
The father as he is? as others did?
Am I not greater than all earthly Kings?
He spake our fathers, wherefore is he hid
That I cannot behold him? Let his wings
Be folded for a while, as he comes down,
That we may see him as he is ; we came
To choose a god, whom we, indeed, can see;
Or, if his face be burnished with a flame
Too great for our uncovered eyes, then we
Are satisfied to close them in the smile
Of one so radiant; so we feel him near,

"But we must know his presence for the while ;
Speak Kohen ! why can ye not bring him here ? "

Then answered Kohen: "Urge me not, O King !
Ye know not what ye ask, if ye do seek
To see him as he is.   A nameless thing,
A brow-bedabbled man, upon whose cheek,
Sheds everyday God's sunshine; shall he ask
That a decree be broken, and presume
To lift unhallowed voice?   Though in a mask
Jehovah hides his presence, yet, the bloom
Of every flower, is but the blush he brings
Upon the face of nature, as he looks
Abroad upon his creatures; and she sings
From her ten thousand voices in his praise.
Wake to his chorus !   ' Ancient of the Days,'
Wake children ! and your faith shall blossom into wings."

" Prate ye to fools," the incensed Monarch cries,
" Nor gabble longer of your hidden Lord ;
Who follows in his wake, this moment dies,
And Isis and eternal keep my word.
We have a score of hidden deities
And yet, they leave us, without aid or thought,
And pestilence comes in and blocks our ways
And where can our deliverence be bought?
Show the bare hand of infinite decree,
Show us a present help in each distress,
Show us the Master, we will bend the knee,

"And we will follow on, in righteousness.
Strike! strike the chords! while we invoke the gods,
And with the music let our souls be blended,
That we may find the one, before whom nods
'All stripling deities, and thus our strife be ended.'"
Then rose a blast of sound upon the air
And blended with it was the voice of song,
The chime of music with the moan of prayer— .
A nation's thirst ; deep, earnest and impassionately strong:

O God of gods!   be with us when we pray,
  And give us rest ;
List our entreaty, be not far away,
  Be near each breast.

The gods of Mizraim, we have sought in vain,—
  They answer not ;
Our prayers are but an empty, aching pain,—
  We are forgot.

Though Isis bless our fields and flocks with growth,
  And Thoth be heard ;
Upon the tongues of wisemen, yet, is wroth
  Some mighty lord.

Some hidden power without us; in the dark
  We grope our way ;
From thine own glory, lend to us a spark,
  Be thou our day.

O, make thee to be known,
From thy unchanging throne,
   God of the trusting heart ;
Come take us by the hand,
And be our sole command,
   And form with us a part.

Give us, to look upon
Thy form without a frown,
   Our doubts and fears displace ;
God of the universe,
Remove from us, thy curse,
   Give us to see thy face.

" Behold ! behold, his face ! "
A hand is pointed to the sun ;
" Behold ! and be ye not afraid,
To-day, be life, once more begun ;
Look ye upon his face, and learn to live,
Look ye upon his face and learn to die ;
His hand alone deliverance can give,
His light, alone, can frame the soul's reply.
' Hear me ! ye sons of men'; all eyes were turned ;
A stranger in their midst, whose dark eye burned
With an unearthly gleam, yet black as night.
It had no heavenly radiance, yet, was bright
With a mysterious blaze, that pierced the soul
As with an arrow to its inmost part,
His form, in keeping with his face, made whole

" A man well fitted to command ; a heart
That seemed to throb with some great passion ; pent
And seething into purpose; his black face
Shone like a mirror-hood of his design.
His words, and his strange presence in the place
Gave him enraptured audience, that no one dared decline.

" Hear me, ye sons of men : I am not come
To woe ye to destruction ; but, to save ;
The color of my face betrays my birth,
I am Mizraim's race ; but of mankind
A brother, and I speak in soberness.
Because our fathers wandered from the way,
And left the shining pathway of the sun,
Because they fell to seeking other gods,
He suffered them to fall into yonr hands.
I will not speak, as he has feigned to speak,
Who claimed before me, sponsorship from God ;
But I will make it plain that he deceived.
Our fathers tell of Noah and the ark,
And also tell of Shinar, and the time
Of the dispersal.   It is not enough
To come with empty declamation, come
With platitudes of love, and softened terms
Of parenthood, and then to dash it all—
The yearning love of children, to the earth,
By words that are icicled up from death :
' Ask not to look upon my face again,
Ye cannot look and live.'

"Shame ! shame on the pretender thus to bring
Your expectations to the pitch of pain,
The summit of your hope, where, to move on
Is only to descent and sorrow ; thus
To multiply his attributes of good,
And to describe a god so like the true,
The ever shining Sun, and then deny
The precious boon of sight ; what mockery !
When there he stands, (eternity, as young,)
The broad, full shining orb, to look upon ;
The ever radiant Arbiter of earth,
The great ' I am ' of love ; the very soul
Of tenderness ; rising every morn
To kiss his sleeping children from their beds,
Enwrapping them, with all his piercing warmth ;
Wooing the fragrant flowers from the earth,
And warming all existences to life.

"How can the soul be blind, when such a pledge
Stands in eternal witness of its love ?
The very rocks would break their raptured trance,
If man find not his voice in fervent praise.
How do the waters mirror up his face !
And tremble into waves at his advance.
The universe goes laughing into life
Each morn at his approach, and all the world
Forgets its wakefulness, when the tired wing
Of day is folded, and himself withdraws

"'To teach us faith in him till he return;
Thus every night his promise, and each morn
His gracious fulfillment, filling the year
With ripened sheaves of his remembrances.

" We measure power by our necessities;
Let him forget the dawning of one day,
Or leave us through the circle of one moon,
(Which were the same to him but for his love,)
By what conception would we feel our loss?
While yet the year is young, we scatter seed,
And wait his fervid rays to fructify.
The trees put forth their bloom, that his embrace
May ripen into fruit; and not a growth
But climbs his rays to full development.
When Nature points with her ten thousand hands
To him, the almighty framer of it all,
Shall man forget his duty and fly off
On the unnumbered tangents of the brain?
Rather let break our voices in his praise,
And let each human soul, be safely borne,
Back to his many-chambered paradise.

" Down on his rays man rode into the world,
And if we wander not, the same broad path
Is open for our exit; there is room
In his broad campus for the royal race.
Our bodies are of dust, and will return;
Only the vital spark, the shining way

" Ere traversed ; and that alone goes back
To join the maker in the increate,
The golden chambers of eternal light.
Look on these eyes ! have they not more than Earth
In their deep glance?   I know whereof I speak ;
For I was led, in trancehood to the sun,
And in his very chambers have I walked,
And at his very throne have I bent down
To praise him ; multitudes were there, who knelt
As I did kneel, in rapturehood and prayer.

" High in the midst, sole source of life and light,
The glowing center of the shining orb
Sat the unchanging god ; his face was that
Of manhood magnified ; upon his cheek
Was more than woman's beauty deified.
    O ! once to look and live, is all the soul,
Though it be triply strengthened, can endure,
Till it do pass from this clay tenement
Into the morrow of the upper world ;
But we may now and always climb the rays
That spring from his own countenance, and see
The reflex of his face ; but of his form,
But little can be printed on our sight.
Enough, to know he lives, and is our life,
And every morning he doth search us out,
And lift the burden from our heavy lids,
That we may rise with him and to our tasks !

"Shall we be hushed, when every bird and flower
Doth herald his approach?   Convolvulus
Waits for his coming with its lips apart,
And Philomela will not close his note,
Till he do answer with his smiling face;
Thus the whole earth resolvent into song
Waits for his footsteps—how can we be dumb!

    "There was a song
Which flowed, untutored, from the lips of love,
The ransomed ones that knelt before his throne,
No earthly tongues its echo could repeat,
So much there was of love, so much of joy,
So much of tenderness and innocence ;
For they were without guile, and not a word
But breathed of faith, dependency and peace.
It praised him for his sufference of earth,
That he did bear its sin, yet did not smite;
And only once, in anger, hid his face,
And oped the heavens, to wash out its filth;
Yet, with his fervent rays, drank up the flood,
And set his bow a witness that again
Never should earth be flooded, while the years
Melt into centuries, till the whole race,
With aching hearts and scalding eyes shall come
Back to his all-embracing fatherhood.

"They thanked him for his witness-watch of man,
That time and time, his face was partly hid,

"To show the hazard of our wandering steps,
That in the early, and the latter rain,
He wept for our refreshment, till his tears
Shut out his fervent glances from our eyes;
And though he mourned our strangerhood of him,
Yet would he teach us that in smiles and tears
Are we begotten, and our lives are lost
If we find not the blessings that are hid
Beneath the rainbow tints of sorrowing.

"Thus much, and more, that I will not essay;
But I was led through fields and garden walks,
And ornate grandeur, which the earth affords
Nor pattern nor approach; and though the mind
Be forced to utmost tension, it cannot
Encompass the bewilderment of sight.
Since my return, I cannot cast it off,
It lingers with me like some raptured dream,
And in my eyes and on my face is drawn
The print of its unspeakable surmount;
And I would call it dream, if I had not
A talisman, that tells me of its truth.
An angel led me to the central throne,
An angel led me back to consciousness;
But ere he passed the confines of the sun,
He handed me a clear, transparent gem,
And called me: ' Uri, thus it shall be said:
The very god commands that it be done;

" 'Uri, my light, my fire upon the earth,
Shall build again my altars and restore
With his own hand, the priesthood of the sun.
I will a hundredfold return the scorn
Of Mizraim on himself, for his neglect;
And from the sons of Lud I will raise up
A kingdom that shall shine in righteousness.'

"This said, he handed me the talisman;
Which, when our altars shall have been prepared,
And laden with the choicest of our flock,
Shall claim the pledge of the eternal one,
With fire from his own courts to burn it up.

" I can not say how long, or short a time,
I lingered thus entranced; I only know
I waked to find it real. The precious gem
Is proof of disenchantment; it is here.

I lay no claim on priesthood, but have told
The plain, uncumbered truth; when I did fall,
Prone to the earth in trance, I had no thought,
Of what would come of it; you have it all.
I have the stone, and we will test its power.
If yonder priest, with his enshrouded myth,
Desires to measure lances with the sun,
Then we will each build altars to our gods,
And he that first draws fire from any source,
Not of the earth, shall claim the forfeiture
Of all the other's tenantry to teach.

"I may have said too much; I can not more
Than leave the rest with god, the changeless one,
The bright, all-shining universe of love,
The unfailing source, the broad, unvarying stream,
The very oceanhood of deity."

He ceased; and Kohen, rising to his feet,
    Gave back the challenge eagerly; as might
The athlete spring his ready foe to meet;
    His, was the conscious power of fearless right:
"Let him lift up his altars to the sun,
And I will call upon the Uncreate,
The hand, that shaped it from chaotic void,
The face, whose look first taught it how to smile.
He may call first, that it may vantage him;
But other than the earth can no man bring,
Fire from the distant realms, except it be
From God, Creator of the sun, the moon and stars.
I am content that he do cry his god,
Till he be hoarse with hardihood of prayer,
This day shall judge between us and the right,
And ye shall see the bare arm of the Lord."

The crowd, impatient of his words, did shout
    In Uri's acclamation; as the sun,
Full-faced and warm, gave back his witnesshood;
    His ready conquest had been well begun.
How few there be, who see beyond their sight !
    Even in our day of peculence and power,

The horizon of man has been his might,
Beyond his ready reach he passes into night;
 The world is bounded by its present hour.
No marvel that old Uri swept the field ;
 His snare was baited for their ready sense,
No effort theirs, a pleasure but to yield;
Theirs but the open book, to them unsealed;
 They felt no weight of future recompense;
And so they shouted, high and loud, his praise,
 "Till he recalled them, with his magic voice:
"Old Kohen seems in earnest; let us raise
 Our altars quickly, that we may rejoice
This day, in our great father's warm embrace,
That we may look unblushing in his face
And call his fervent rays to their full test
Ere he shall draw the curtain in the west."

So said, so done; two altars were soon reared,
Both prophets, in full confidence appeared;
The offerings have been brought; and now they wait
 Only the word; the King must give command.
Against gray Kohen, was the leveled fate
 Of his unsolaced anger; yet, his hand
Was stayed by counsel, and he only said,
 "Uri calls first, let every breath
Be hushed upon his calling. Let the dead
 From out their cerements beneath
Bear witness with our spirits that we seek

" A true solution to the psalm of life.
Slay thou the offering, Uri, and then speak,
    Speak the charmed word, and close the strife."

Uri comes forth and in one hand he brings
The talisman with leathern circlet stayed,
Enclosing surfaces convex; to this he clings
As though the whole earth in the balance laid,
Were mean in weight compared to such a gem.
The other holds a knife, and with a stroke
The offering is prepared; he looked at them,
The thirsting, hungry eyes that watch, then broke
The silence, turning full upon the sun:
" Thy will, most radiant god! thy will be done.
O shining face! of the unchanging one,
Look, in the pity thou alone canst feel
And lead us back to life, we claim thy pledge.
A nation, lifts to thee their centered prayer;
They see thy smile, they know thy heart of hearts.
They hush them here, upon their altar's brink,
For they can go no nearer; meet, thou, them,
And, as we look upon thy face, may we
Behold thy very presence in our midst;
Come as a flame, to lick this offering up,
And all our hearts shall melt into thy smile."

He raised the gem before the flaming sun;
The rays concentered, and the flames burst forth

As leaping to their master.   'Twas enough.
The multitude, in thought, became as one.
And all, save Kohen, sank upon their knees;
And whispers of relief, fell on the breeze.
They were as pliant clay in Uri's hands,
And hung upon the breath of his commands:
" Pour forth your homage, chosen of the sun,
Once more his warmth encloses; and we feel
Responsive throbbings of his fatherhood.
Rise and rejoice!" Their ready voices raise
From lips, new touched in unison of praise.

Old Kohen was confounded at the first.·
He had not thought it possible, to bring
Fire from the sun, or any mortal thing;
No shadow of its secret on him burst;
But he had heard of sorcery and arts
Among the sons of Mizraim, and not long
Before the lion of his nature starts,
In cold defiance of the clamorous throng,
To slay his offering; and his lips poured out
The very thunder-throe of earnest prayer;
A fervency that would not harbor doubt,
That ever is a stranger to despair.
Long, earnest, loud and fervently, he prayed;
And his gray locks ensilvering the breeze,
Gave pathos, to the torrent thus unstayed;
Yet, not for self, did he the angel seize;

But wrestled for his people thus misled.
" Unscale their eyes, O Father!" so he pled.
" Unstop their ears, O thou, All Powerful One
That they may hear thy footfall on the wind.
Come in thy flame, and purge them with thy fire.
Strike off the fetters from their prisoned souls !
Make me an offering for their flagrant sins,
And I will bare my bosom to the knife,
And bend my neck in cheerfulness to thee,
So thou wilt save my people from the hand
Of this misguided witch of Mizraim!"
His prayer had hardly ceased, ere shot the flame,
From upper zenith, down, and in one glow,
Pierced the whole altar with impetuous claim,
And lapped the other with its overflow.
The crowd, transfixed with wonder at the scene,
Could hardly trust the witness of their eyes,
And held divided counsels, till the King
Quenching the current of their late surprise,
Poured his recruited anger on Kohen.

" Why longer parley, with a thing so plain ?
    Old Kohen had no warrent for this deed;
The palm was Uri's who did rightly gain
    Fire from the sun, to him alone, we plead ;
He drew it first, old Kohen must admit,
    And he should paid due homage to our god ;
And from what source did his become enlit ?

"We serve no phantom, with its hidden nod,
But look upon the face of him we serve ;
    The sun has kept his fire for us these years,
And we, his children, never can deserve
    His untold blessings; though our prayers and tears,
Should mingle with each altar that we raise
    In all the future ages, still our debt
Will always be uncancelled by our praise
    And all our past be covered with regret.
We want no juggling on this sacred day,
    That gives us back the father, we had lost.
Bind old Kohen, and hasten him away,
    He shall repay his treachery with cost.
To-morrow shall another altar grace
    This precious grove, made sacred to the sun,
And Kohen shall be offered in this place,
    To pay the sacrilege he had begun."

In thy own way our Father ; we must wait
    So many times, because we cannot see ;
Yet thou alone canst bring us to the gate,
    How slowly do we learn to trust in thee !
Yet, in withholding, are the blessings hid,
    As frequent as in giving ; all our prayers
If they result in doing but thy bid,
    Will scatter diamond dust above our cares.
The gray old Prophet murmured : "Let God's will
    Be done, and in abeyance I will bare my breast,

" I will not doubt him though indeed he kill,
  His chosen way must surely be the best."

The morrow came and at the King's command
  The multitude assembled, and the guard
Brought forth the Prophet, looking proudly grand
  As some great warrior claiming his reward
Of beys and laurels, wreathed into a crown;
  They rear the pile and he awaits his doom
Without a menace, and without a frown.
Then turning to the press : " I will assume
Your hearts are mine, my sons, I know it well;
Your eyes beheld the witness of our God,
And greatly were ye moved ; but 'tis his will
That I should join my fathers in that land,
Where canker and corruption never comes,
The why, and wherefore of it, is his own ;
I bow my head in thankfulness to him,
That he has deemed me worthy to exchange
A life of sorrow for a crown of love.

" Ye are the servants of an earthly King,
And God has suffered him to lead you off,
His will be done ; but I must tell you now
Your future as I read it in the glass
Of my illumined death:
                 " I see the black
Of Mizraim, sweep the brown of Lud from off

The face of Egypt; and I also see
A wandering race, go northward, and to east;
I see a bitter wintering of snow;
I see the sun hide back his face from them;
I see a boisterous buffeting at sea;
I see a journey southward—a new world."

"And centuries flow swiftly on my sight.
A people proudly resting in their wealth ;
The Son of God, in the full flight of years ;
The conquest of the nations in his name.
A proud and prosperous people cross the sea
And swoop upon this nation of the sun ;
Their temples crumble in the hand of God
And he takes back his own. All this I see
As what cannot avert ; it is God's way,
And wisdom is the wastage of his throne.
He cannot order wrongly ; I submit
My wasting image to his waiting hands :
"Come Father ! I am ready."

He raised him to the pile ; with look divine,
He prone himself upon it ; at the sign
The Prophet Uri raised the crystal stone ;
The sun threw down its rays, and shot the flame
Full to the center ; as the altar shone,
Each eye was turned, and every voice was tame,
As down the chancel of the deep blue sky,

A flaming chariot sped, and came a cry :
"It is enough, come higher up ; thou shalt
Not suffer death." A hand, not human, caught
The grand old Prophet ; his recumbent form
Rose on their dazzled sight as rainbow in the storm.

Thus was the error fixed ; and it is well
We leave them to their blindness for a while.
Misguided worship, left alone, will tell
Its own pathetic story : there is guile
To underlie each sorrow of the race.
Fruit comes alone from seed ; somewhere is sown
The germ of every grief, and nature on its face
Bears no repentant feature ; as we plant, so shall the tree
    be grown.

EXPULSION FROM EGYPT.

The seasons pass, till on their hands they count
    Four palms, and to the third, a score and three
In life's meridian how the circles mount
    That measure our existence, if there be
No canker worm that clogs the ready wheel ;
    If care hangs not upon the skirts of time ;
And if, like most mankind, we only feel
    Its gentle passing, by the hills we climb
In ambling, easy way, and retrospect
    Surprises into thought, and we wake up

To feel how swift we journey. We reflect
  After reflection barrens of its fruit, the cup
Which we have mixed we drink ; if it be gall
  We gulp it down the same ; we cannot change
The current of our lives, and useless is the call
  On any but the hand of God. 'Tis strange
The miracle of life should ever pass
  And print no letters deep into the soul !
The years go by, and, but the tuft of grass
  More reverent than we, tells o'er our dust its rosary, in
    deep green scroll.

MIZRAIM AND LUD.

Near the rim of Karoun, where the pyramids drink the
    dew that should dampen the soil ;
And the Nilus pours over its green level banks, its annual
    freightage of spoil ;
Where the date ripens dark to the child of the sun, and
    the pomegranate colors for fruit ;
The ibis is sounding the damps of the land, and earth in
    its plethory mute.

The fat of the fields husks the voice of the morn, while
    Demeter isweighing her sheaves ;
The lotus has honied its lips for the kiss, "and the turtle
    in mockery grieves."
What is that, where the Orient gathers her gold, and the
    eye wanders back to the sea?

What cloud on the horizon's breach can be seen? What
wakens the vulture's rude glee?

' 'Tis the shock of the battle that burdens the air, and
the armies that burden the eye ;
They have met (could Elysian give landscape more
fair ?), have met to embrace and to die.
The Prophet still lives, and has led to the sun all Egypt ;
and gathered as one
The people to hallow the harvest-moon feast, ere the work
of the year is done.

But Mizraim outnumbers the children of Lud, and the
shepherd kings, crafty and weak,
Have laid tasks on their shoulders too heavy to bear, till
the voice of their burden must speak.
In vain the gray Prophet lifts up to his god his winglet of
prayer for peace ;
The tempest of war has broke over the plain, and his altars can bring no surcease.

The black and the bronze, the iron and brass ; how they
struggle and grip for the field !
The spear and the arrow, the halbert and lance, and who
shall be first to yield?
Not the iron ; it is strong and resistless in weight. Not the
brass ; it is beaten and firm.
What a hecate of agony burdens the plain ! what a banquet
for vulture and worm !

But the iron is too heavy, the brass is too thin, and under the weight it gives way,
As a wall, that is breached and toppled by time ; and Mizraim gains the day.

Oppression, when reversed, is double weight ;
The Slave pours lead into the lash he bore ;
And, as the Master adds recruited hate
To blows, that he has learned to feel before,
The soul its letters of forgiveness learns
From only one great Master, in all time ;
Revenge is human, and forever burns
Upon the trackway of retreating crime.
The text and testwork of their lives was lost ;
And when the King was slain, and they o'erthrown,
His people paid their tyranny with cost.

Only the Prophet, with his magic stone,
Could purchase their withdrawal ; they must leave
(They were the early jewels of the sun)
And Uri pledged their fortunes to retrieve,
If they would journey, where the day begun,
And seek the closer presence of their god,
In paths where human feet had never trod.
They must divide with Egypt ; but go out
Well laden for the journey ; should they dare
To turn, the heavy hand of Mizraim would not spare.

Ægyptus ! thou above thy gates hath writ
So many times the monosylbic " when."
We, weary of conjecture ; round us flit
The phantoms of the past ; and we again
Pass in review thy pages, black with mold ;
Intemporate within a crumbling earth,
Against the char of empires thou dost hold
The charms that emulate immortal birth.
We write mutation on the brow of Time ;
Thou art the changeless one of all the world—
Thou hast no brotherhood in any clime;
All mortal barbets have in vain been hurled.

"Time conquers all things ? " Thou giv'st back the lie ;
Above its ruins, thou dost stand, serene—
Eternity !—Must thou, perforce, then die?
What tragedy hast thou, indeed, not seen ?
Must thou, too, look on death ? thou wilt not dim ;
But in impassive slumber, thou wilt fall
As sinks the sun, beneath the horizon's rim,
And answer only the Archangel's call.
We leave thee loathely, for our souls are wed
To thy enchanted gardenhood of lore.
"The morning stars sang joy" above thy bed,
The nations, in their cerements, shall pass thy door,
And earth be wrapped in ashes ere thy brow shall bear
          the fatal legend, " Nevermore."

THE MOURNING SHEPHERDS

The tambour' is silent, O god of the Nile !
The harp has been hung in acacian shade.
We are bowed to the earth, we are broken and bent,
And the blade of our fathers in dust has been laid.

We came, as the simoom creeps over the plain ;
We came, as the tiger its covert forsakes ;
As the hurricane brushes the dust from the brakes ;
As the lightning leaps out and the thunder-god shakes.

We are shorn of our strength as with plague we are smote;
The axe has been wrenched from the hands that are
    brawn,
And the arms whose strong sinews till now were unbent
Have been broken as brittles ; our prowess is gone.

O ! thou bright shining god ! with thy scintles of gold;
If thy children have gathered the glow of thy face,
If thy kisses, ere warmed to the lips that are cold,
O we pray ! let us feel thy impassioned embrace.

We are journeying forth to the cradle of morn,
Where thy lids feel the weight of their slumbering still;
We would kneel at thy bed where the seasons are born,
And learn from thy lips the whole law of thy will.

Have we sinned in thy sight ? have we slackened our pace ?
Are we paying the forfeit in wormwood of shame ?

We draw nearer to thee, and our lives we would place
  In the hands of the Maker, that out of thy flame

We may gather that fire that shall glow with thy love ;
  And will never grow dim through the future of years,
That shall make us like thee, and our fealty prove
  "Till we learn to forget this dark trackhood of tears.

As we turn to the East, wilt thou smile on our way ?
  Wilt thou lessen the distance between us and thee ?
Or our hearts remain hungry, the shadow still stay
  With its wizard arm lifted to smite as we flee.

We doubt thee no longer--we know thou wilt aid ;
  We turn to the path where thy morning rays shine ;
We will seek thy first footfall, and all unafraid,
  We feel thee, we love thee, we know we are thine.

We leave the old life, with the graves of our kin,
  We turn from the sunset of dampness and death,
We turn where the light with its god doth begin,
  And the praise of the day-king embalms every breath;

Where the sun slakes his thirst with the dew of the flow-
      ers,
  Where the night flees before him far into the west,
Where the honey-dew clingsto the fruit-laden hours,
  Where the soul sets its table, with Joy as its guest.

So does our faith stand out against our grief ;
So does our hope grow up into belief.

One God? Yes, Father, Thou! and only One.
We praise thee ; yet, our praise is only done,
When we extol thee for the gift of faith.
Not every one can name thee ; but each breath
May be enladen with the thought of praise
And all adore thy attributes—the ways
That they adore thee are not always thine ;
Yet, do they bend to thy great thoroughfare and shine
With light from the Eternal throne ; 'tis well,
Nor otherwise than good—it can but swell
The choral of thy praise ; and in the end
These thousand thoughts of Deity, in thee, not fail to
   blend.

THE JOURNEY.

O thou ! who charmed the demons in the breast
Of Saul, and set the universal voice
Of all the earth to thy unflagging song ;
Thou royal shepherd ! bend for us across
The bridge of ages thy leant lips, and pour
The echo of thy music on_our souls.

And Thou of Nazareth ! whose very life
Was as the cadence of a well-strung harp,
Thyself the instrument, upon whose strings,
Ten thousand symphonies are left entranced ;
Pour in the empty vial of our verse,
Some of thy soul of music, and let shine

Through every darkened crevice of the heart,
Rays of celestial sunshine.   Not in vain
Our humble dalliance, if thou set the charm
Of thine approval.   Let our song be praise
And devotate our hands, that there be left
No tissue, but is animate of Thee !

The seas reach out to clasp each other's hands,
The greater and the less, and leap the sands
That tear in two their waters ; but not so
She of the Nile ; her rights will not forego.
The hand that rocks the crib of empire holds
A charm, that locks the East and West in one
The track of nations is her beaten path,
And undisputed, till the earth be done.
Man may disturb it, but the hand of God
Has placed a thousand tokens on this sod.

The flocks are gathered, and the flight began,
Old Uri and attendants in the van ;
The portents were of good as far as seen,
Each breast a shrine of hope ; thus early man
Gave little time to sorrow — after years
Were left for its fruition ; light of heart,
These early-planted germlets of the earth,
Took their reverses in the better part
Of hardihood ; they had thus early learned,
That in the chafe of fortune there is gain ;

That scars are coronets, though they be burned
Deep in the brow of care; each gem a pain.
Our philosophic age with heavy draught,
Drinks deep in phantasies, but fails to learn
The wiser lesson of this early craft,
To catch the wheel of fortune with each turn.

East over Syria they bent their steps,
    Meeting Euphrates many leagues above
Where Babylon since molded into form
    Her mystical proportions ; and so strove
Persistently the mastery of earth.
    Crossing the Tigris but a span below,
Where Taurus from his fountains feeds the stream,
    They traverse Persia with its after-glow
Of conquest ; where Ispahan gave touch,
To chords that deify the voice of song,
And mellow through the ages, if so much
As but an echo would inspire the tongue,
With that enchantment, that rolls down the course
Of her great history. We seek in vain
Another Cyrus, or another force
Of Scripture fulfillment, with lesser pain,
And Time's repleted garner has no riper grain.

Still East they cross the Amoo, and above
Where now, Bokhara's languor and repose
Invites the Sclavic hordes in summer quest
Of forage. And Belor, giant like, still throws

Its shadow o'er the landscape ; and the Koosh
Shortens the noon of summer, from the South ;
A thousand sparkling torrents downward rush,
And pour their waste of waters in the mouth
Of Indus. They cross where Belor melts its snow,
To placid Cashgar's arms, sending below
A current to the waste of farther Nor.
They stand on Cobis' southern girt, and drink
The final retrospective of the West ;
And keep the gloomy borders to the brink
Of far-off Koulon, where the Argoon lends
Its mite of wastage to the vast Amour ;
And the impetuous Shilka, swiftly sends
Its tribute to the master of Mantchoor.

One winter they had spent upon the way,
Within the vale of Cashgar, where the flocks
Found generous herbage ; but they could not stay
Longer than opening spring, when from the rocks
And passes of the Koosh, a savage tribe
Came fiercely on them ; and again the fire
From Uri's sacred pebble, as a bribe
Saved them from ruin, and the warlike ire
Of Lama's devotees, for even then
On upper Ind, his worship had begun ;
But superstition, ranks us all as men,
And mystery doth mold us into one.

The Argoon and the Shilka passed ; they keep
Their steady march, down Armour's limpid tide.
Yet summer wastes to autumn.   Seasons creep
So noiselessly, that our souls are open wide,
If we set watch upon them; unaware
They find us napping, in our wakeful age ;
And how much more, in the unrisen sun
Of ancient man ! We wonder that the page
Is not more blurred and blotted in the years
That are far gone, when knowledge only bubbled up
    through tears.

A Winter on the Amour near the sea ;
The Frost King strokes his heavy beard in glee,
In surfeit of his triumph, o'er the foe
That dares invade his borders ; and the snow
Scatters its fleecy fullness o'er the land,
Hiding the face of Nature with its hand
So cold and clasping.   O 'tis very hard !
To see familiar faces pass the ward
Of our immediate contact, and the earth
Draw back into its arms, with tightening girth
Our loved ones.   But 'tis a heavier lot
To see our mother Earth, whose faithful breast
Has never failed to aid ; so chilled in death
That it cannot respond, though it be rest,
Recuperent and needful ; still the same
When we are starving for its warm caress,

And cannot spare its nursing, when our claim
Is mortal, and we feel the strong hand press
Our vitals ; and we labor for our breath ;
And Famine lends its wizard hand, to fill the tooth of
    death.

Old Uri vainly calls the shining god ;
    Though it may light his altar, still the flame
Is but a weakling ; and the weary host
    Were wrangling at his impotence, and tame
His efforts to assuage them. He had taught
    His followers of a near approach ; the sun
Seemed coy of his endeavors, for the thought
    Of zone or solstice, had not then begun,
And Winter was their time of penance, when
    Their god rode low, and frowned him out of sight.
They offered for his anger many gifts,
    And set their watchmen to outwake the night.
In question of his rising. Why should he
    Keep so much closer the horizon's rim
When they were in his quest, and sought the verge
    Of farthest empire, in their reach of him ?
O empty arms ! and ever reaching out,
    Fold in the blessings that your hands enclose.
There is nor reason, nor excuse for doubt,
    The river of God's love so near you flows.
Your very feet are on the water's brink,
    His very arms are all around you thrown,

You touch him in your timidness, and shrink
To his embraces; no human soul was ever yet alone.

They settle down to Winter, and their flocks
Must furnish sustenance, until the sun
Shall break their penance, and embrown the locks
Of the o'ergristled seasons ; and this won,
They counsel further movement.   Uri speaks :
"Sons of the Summer God, I little thought
When we set out from Egypt, that our feet
Would be thus bruised and bled ; but it is well.
We learn the lesson of our latent sin;
This trial of our faith will make us whole,
If we but draw the diamond out of it.
We have not vainly trod the heavy press
Of our affliction, if we firmly breast
The waters.   I have kept faithful watch—
We are but self-styled lords, and forfeit much
Of our asserted masterhood ; the birds
Make many less mistakes—we used to note
The flight of waterfowl in Egypt.   Why
Should we not learn their wisdom in this clime?
Before the sun sank low, and Winter came
(Led by a providence that makes all things
To minister our wants), I watched the birds,
And many, turned to East, across the sea.
We lose our way sometimes, they never do ;
They are much closer children to the sun

Than we, by their dependence—we need help
As much as any feathered wingster does—
And yet we push it back, when we might reach
And find a steady hand.   Let us go to
And make us ships ; that when the Spring
Shall beckon back to life the dormant earth,
And all the birds turn back in countermarch,
We fly against their flight, and reach the clime
From whence the sun has warned them to return
To this cold country of the nether earth.

" Behold ! these rugged trees stand stout for us,
And ready for our architrave ; and we
Were better wont to labor than to dole
Our time in murmurs at our fate.   Up ! up !
And do ! and though we suffer overmuch,
Our labor shall not vainly mock at us.
Even old Kohen saw a journey South,
When he did burn our eyes, as he went up,
And he saw fat and plenty in the land
Where his prophetic eye did cast our lot ;
And we will not mistrust what leads to light,
Though it be lifted in a demon's hand."

The forests gave to them their virgin palms,
    And they did rudely shape them into crafts ;
Made ready for the flood, when the warm sun
    Should waken nature with enlivening draughts ;

But Spring wore into Summer, ere the birds
   Gave the unspoken pledge of their return.
The sun, still coy, refused to climb as high
   As it had done in Egypt ; still they burn
With new-born hope, as they float down to sea,
   And, moving counter to their winged friends,
Cross to Lopatka, where they only wait
   Replenishment, which nature always sends,
Where faith is instinct as in lower life,
   (The birds teach providence, without a chance,)
And so they wander on, to the Aleutes ;
   Passing and calling, as they still advance,
They reach to where Alaska strikes the sea,
   In severance to meet them.   They kept on,
Feeding on eggs of seabirds, and the meats
   That everywhere supplied them.   They have gone
So far on Nature's very track, and now
   A narrow river beckons their research,
And they pass upward, till a mountain range
   Confronts their passage, like a royal perch
From which the gods might frown their hardihood,
   For this intrusion of another world.
But they have battled with the plague and flood ;
   And though Olympus all his thunders hurled,
They had not turned ; they saw the earnest need
   Of pushing forward ere the sun turned back,
And so they crossed to where the eastern slope,
   Feeds the McKenzie.   Here an easy track

Leads down and cuts the stronger range in two,
   A little while among its shadows grope,
When the broad prospect opened to their view.
   They follow the receding sun in hope,
Still bearing to the east their steady trend,
Hoping to win their God to close embrace ;
And morn and eve around their altars bend
In thankfulness, that they still see his face.
Through many valleys, virgin to their sight,
And many lakes, whose bosoms never stirred
To man, the weak pretender of God's might ;
But nature spreads her happy hearth with beast and
    flower and bird.

PART SECOND.

AZTLAN.

THE VALLEY OF THE MISSISSIPPI.

Father of Waters ! Nilus of the West !
  Thou holdst thy secrets from the sons of men ;
A knowledge of the past which none would wrest
  Or wish to circumscribe with tongue or pen
To the weak bonds of history ; but rather stand
With old De Soto on thy banks, and reverence the hand
That drew the fetters from 'thy limbs, and set thee first
    at birth,
On thy unmuzzled pilgrimage, without a peer on earth.

Better thy unbroke seal, if it would teach
The ponderous worm of destiny, called man ;
How great things may be hidden from his reach,
And mighty things be silent, that his span
Is but a hand-breadth to the great unknown,
A thistle-down, before the breezes blown,
That silent and unseen God turns the mighty mill,
And on the brow of giant force he writes his words,
    " Be still."

The possibles of time, are all thine own.
Thou hast not reared thy monuments of stone

To overtop the pyramids, yet wrought
In shapely mounds, thy sculpturehood, and caught
From flying Time, the lustre of his wing,
Which gives the semblance of perpetual Spring
To thy vast lap of luxuries; in thee
(Since man first pinioned thee to history)
Is found the acme of a world's desire.
Thy unknown crucial test, has passed the fire
Of many fading centuries; let none inquire
The secrets of thy conquest: be thou shut up with God,
The master molding of his hand—the jewel of his rod !

Yet in the book of Nature there is writ,
Without exception, all her energies,
As line by line, her page becomes enlit;
Yielding to man some new and glad surprise,
As Agassiz, together works with her,
To make the earth, her own interpreter;
And such a giant, must not hope to hide
The unfading Sanscrit, written on its side.

Thy brow wast glistered with the frost of years,
Ere man's first rapture, at the sight of thee ;
Yet, were thy banks unswelled, by falling tears
Till he tore back thy splendid tapestry—
The bison and the deer unfrighted came
To lave upon thy borders, all were tame,
In their untoilsome frolics ; and the beasts and birds
Made rolic at thy feet, in songs not marred with words.

But sorrow comes with knowledge; 'tis the tree,
That bears the samest fruit in every zone—
The tale of Eden is no mystery,
The tree will verify wherever grown.
And yet, in God's own providence 'tis best,
That Eden be repeated East and West ;
If knowledge in the first, brought sorrowhood to earth,
The power to laugh and cry, were purchased at one birth.

They stand upon thy borders: Mighty Stream !
We will not pry thy silent lips apart,
To ask thee when, and how, the Prophet's dream
Reached its fulfillment ; treasured in thy heart,
Let it remain as many other things
Are left ; our language lessens their effect,
And makes them small in words,—the very springs
Of our existence, are not shown correct,
When crowded into verbage,—so we lay
Our beys upon thee, and we feel 'tis thine ;
Thine every secret, of the grand emprise,
With only one unlicensed hand, the Hand of the Divine.

It is enough that after waste and want
And weariness of spirit they have found
A rest upon thy margin, that thy arms
Are opened to enclose them, and the sound
Of human voices mingle with the notes
Of myriad waterfowl. The thousand throats
Of thy unmeasured pasture, blend in praise

To the All Father for the countless ways
That point his providence. The raven's cry
Strikes never vainly, thy omniscient ear,
No effort, but is answered " here am I,"
No prayer but finds the parent very near.

The unconscious hallelujahs of the plain,
The untaught praises of the lofty trees,
The waving upward palms of laden grain,
The mellow notes upon the evening breeze,
The " reveillies " from off the mountain tops,
The nightingale's "tattoo," the many lips
Touched only once by God, the faithful drops
    That wear unceasing at the granite mine,
The praise that never sinks to prayer, the finger tips
    That span the universal zone of life ; all, all incline
To adoration.   If we lose our way
    (As these poor souls had done) we need but turn
To catch the choral of the passing day.
    Behold on every branch and beam the altars burn !
And all things beckon us of God, if we but bend
    The enquiring ear, and catch the keynote of the
        mighty song
That swells from all the universe; we too may blend
    In the vast concord, happiest of the throng.

The rhythmal of the angels, is not far
    From the first prattle of the infant's tongue- -

Both caught the glitter of the Eastern star;
  The harps were both, by the same Master strung ;
The glory of the one, glows from the face;
    The other lifts, to meet its parent's kiss.
    Not very far, the border land of bliss,
From every infant of the human race.
  The sacred fane of childhood, when first reared,
How like a prophecy it should be read—
  A thing to be adored, and sometimes feared!
So many unseen hands, smooth down the bed
  Of infancy ; we can but jostle with our utmost care
Against angelic presences that bend
  And print their unseen kisses on the brow,
And with the infant earth, the Heavenly essence blend.

The wheel that never tires, and ever turns,
  Crushing the neck of nations in its round,
Before whose tread, the star of empire burns,
  Behind whose trend, the ridged and furrowed ground
Gives mute quiescence, to the Master hand ;
  This wheel rolls on ; and now upon thy banks
Great River of the West the infant's cry
  Is mingled with the forest din; thy ranks
Are opened to admit the "lullaby"
  Of earth's last entity ; thou did'st not groan
When buffalo and beaver found thy side,
  Nor when thy trees, first echoed to the moan
Of the despondent turtle, to his bride ;

And thou did'st smile on this invading race,
And open thy broad prairies, as the palm
    Of some great hearted giant, to embrace
The sea-tossed wanderers, the healing balm
    Of thy great heaving breast, rubbed almost out
The wrinkles from the faces of these sires
    Of early Egypt; they forgot the drought
And mildew of their wanderings, and the fires
    Of their thanksgiving altars, gave a zest
They never yet had felt ; an empire spread
    Around them, in the flush of its full growth
A bride, inviting the espousal bed.

Their ranks had been depleted ; yet a few
    Still lingered with the Prophet, who had stood
At the first altar ; when the fervent sun
    First answered their entreaty, and the blood
Was lapped by solar flame; and now, that peace
    Enshrines their hearts, and plenty spreads their board,
They warm towards their leader, and return
    To their old-fashioned loyalty ; his word
Is sacred as the smiling of the sun
    Whose burnished mirror likenesses their forms,
And in whose bosom after life is done,
    The weary find a shelter from all storms.
Nor do they want a psalmist for his praise,
    But he is found with ready harp and voice,
To turn the multitude, with rapturous gaze,

Upon the god of their unshaken choice.
Their morning song is mingled with the mirth,
    That rolics from the sycamore and oak,
The song that swells the green and fruent earth,
    That needs no trumpet's blare, nor kettle stroke.

THE MORNING SONG OF THE MOUND BUILDERS.

Once more do we turn on thy face our glad eyes,
    Great god of the Summer ! and sing,
With the lark and the linnet we gladly arise
    To welcome the smile of our King.

Our hearts are made glad when we feel thee advance
    On thy mission of mercy and might,
For we know that the stroke of thy conquering lance,
    Has shattered the bulwarks of night.

We look on they face, and our doubts are dispelled
    By the glance of thy mellowing eye;
For we feel that the rains by our Master are held,
    And we fear not to do or to die.

We felt thy embrace, many long weary years,
    Yet the scales were not torn from our eyes;
We sought for a father, with prayers and with tears
    Till we woke with a welcome surprise.

And beheld from thy face, *all* the fatherhood shine,
    And thy great glowing heart *all* ablaze

With the love, that had lingered and grown more divine,
  In the yearn of our wandering days.

How we leaped to thy arms, when we saw them extend!
  How we drank of thy fervent embrace!
With its love like thyself, glowing on without end,
  In the gold of thy deified face.

For our eyes were unscaled, and our hearts were unsealed;
  We were melted to tears at the thought,
Of the blessings so near, that had stood unrevealed,
  Of the Providence waiting unsought.

How could we have lost the firm grasp of thy hand,
  With its daily improvise of love,
With its unsounded depths, like the count of the sand,
  As an index, to point us above?

And now hover o'er us, great god of the day!
  Let us never escape from thy wing,
For ever and ever, drive famine away,
  Give wealth to our Summer and Spring.

Give us harvests of fruit, give us Winters of rest—
  Let thy Provident hand never cease;
Grant the aged a home, on thy great shining breast,
  When their labors shall purchase release.

Be more than we ask, give us more than our prayer—
  All our wants, let thy wisdom disclose,
Till our souls shall be ripe with thy fostering care,
  And made white for our future repose.

THE EVENING THANKSGIVING AND PRAYER.

Sinking down to thy rest,
In the deep crimson West,
Great God ! thou hast taught us repose;
With thy promised return,
Without doubting, we learn,
To wait for thy further disclose.

In thy tenement high,
Blazing over the sky,
Are thy sentinels, pledge of the night;
And we know by their shine,
That thy care is divine,
And we rest without fear, till the light

Springs again from the East
With its glory increased
By the wakening pulse of the day;
And we never will doubt,
That thy naked arm, stout,
Will drive all the shadows away.

Yet we cannot forebear,
To lift up our prayer,
For we know we are wanton and weak;
And if once thou shouldst fail,
Or thy face shouldst grow pale,
Where else in the world should we seek ?

For a father so kind,
To a people so blind,
In our weakness, thy strength we may trace.
Then fail not to return,
Leave us never to mourn.
The wealth of thy daily embrace.
O continue, we pray,'
To bring back the glad day ;
Give us always, to look on thy face !

The trembling lisp of every human soul,
    Of names more potent, then their own can be,
Breathes the same lesson through, from pole to pole
    To prove the certitude of Deity.
Not every eye turned upward can behold
    The face that faith alone shapes into form ;
Not every hand can touch the gates of gold
    That outward swing in welcome from the storm.
Yet is the " Abba Father " pendant from each tongue,
    And every soul a furnace for its fires ;
And sacred is each song in earnest sung,
    When creature to Creator thus aspires.
We blindly grope in this, our broad of day,
    The two eternities to thus unite ;
The silk of infancy is turned to gray
    Ere we have learned to tread the path aright.
We force our providences out of reach,
    Throw back the hand our Father doth extend,

And shut our ears that he may vainly teach,
   And all the wealth of heaven may expend
To warm us to reliance,- shall we dare
   To sneer at those who grope? . We grapple air
When it is all refulgent with our God,
   And we may touch his garment's hem in prayer.

THE PROPHET'S DEATH.

Groping in undiscovered realms their way,
The Prophet and his people give the day
To finding safest lodgement, till they press
Well down the grand old river, to the mouth
Of the great Western confluent—the south
Seems to add Summer to the wilderness.

They cross the river, and then settle down
   To love and labor on its grassy banks ;
And fortune seems to have forgot its frown.
   Years of repletion fill their shattered ranks,
And youth and vigor take the place of age ;
   The story of their journey is retold
By only few in number ; and the sage,
   Who turned their faces on their god of gold,
Was bent with the plethoric weight of years,
And summoned them to worship 'mid the tears
Of many, who misgave his failing strength ;
He saw their apprehensions and at length
Called them together for a final word:

" Sons of the Summer God ! it is but wise
That we look out beyond the brace of years,
And question of the future.   All the way
The shining surface of our god has led
Our toilsome footsteps ; we must not forget
His daily nurture, nor the cloth of gold
With which he covers us—wakeful with the day,
How has he touched our eyelids with his hands,
And warmed us with his hovering !   The night
Has never failed his promise of the morn.
How has his parenthood outwatched the stars ;
How has the Winter melted at his glance ;
How has his armor battled with the snows !
With what a tenderness he decks the fields,
And wooes the grasses from the dormant earth,
And clothes the forest with its robes of green,
As covert for the bison and the deer,
That we may find replenishment of food !
His providence has never failed our steps,
Our homage cannot cancel his regard.

" Our father ! in this failing cup of years,
Help us to be re-sanctified to thee—
Thou hast not measured to our helplessness,
But with unstinted hand filled up our lives
With blessings.   Fill thou alike our hearts,
That we may have no room to cherish doubt,
But answer thy embraces, as the fields

Leap up to kiss thy first recumbent rays!
Let all our dross become thy burnished gold,
Shine through each crevice of our stubbornness,
Till in transparent purity, we reach
The very essence of thy godliness!

"Brethren of the Sun!
This altar is my last: You see the fire
Leap as an answer to my late request,
And it shall bear my spirit to the sun,
And cursed the hand that stays its homeward flight!"

Fresh nerved he reached the altar with a bound,
  And sank without a murmur in the flame;
His followers an instant gather round,
  But he had passed out almost as he came.

They did not dare to drag him from the pile,
  His life and effort had together ceased,
He passed into the future with a smile—
  A smile, that he had been so quick released.
Yet, there was one (clear-sighted from the rest),
  Who said she saw the essence of his form,
In brighter effigy, more richly dressed,
  Fly out into the sunset; and the charm
Of her enchanted parable found faith
  In many of the multitude; his death,
So like his life, had challenged all their thought
  And they were ready to quiesce his fate, and sought

Some shadowed miracle to wrap his shade.
　They gathered up the ashes, and forbade
Unsanctioned hands to touch them ; and they reared
　A rugged mound above the garnered dust,
And left him (one whom they loved less than feared).
　To that sole arbitor, whose name is Just,
Our common parent, Time, whose busy hands
　Rear many a sacred fane above our faults,
Flings over our excressences his sands,
　And leaves no human stain to blot the sacred marble
　　of our vaults.

How grand is the economy of time and death !
　We whet the knife for deep incision on the name
Of some misguided leader, but he fails his breath,
　And all our better angels give him back to fame ;
Death carries off the husk, we keep the ripened wheat,
　And Time refines the kernel into choicest flour ;
The atmosphere of anger is at last made sweet;
　Our charity immortal glows ; our passion, but an hour.
God keep us always so !　It is the chosen link
　That binds us to the race, and bids the Christ come in;
That holds our hands to near the eternal brink ;
　It saves us from ourselves, and breaks the tooth of sin.

The whitened garments at the eternal gate,
　Must cover those, who have not stained another,
Or there will come that awful sentence : " Wait !

"Blood crieth from the ground ! where is thy brother?"
If thus upon the living God doth set the seal
Of condemnation for the false witnessing
How will he smite the lips of those who steal
His covering from the dead, and fill the sacred spring
Of memory, with the debris of their lives ;
Mixing, what God has kindly torn apart,
And making null, the severence he strives,
Between the naked soul, and sin encumbered heart !

The gem was melted, and his life went out
In unobtrusive secrecy, and all
That he brought with him, passed the silent way
Into eternity, beyond recall.
He chose no sponsor to renew his place
But gave them back to Nature, as he found ;
Yet was his impress fastened on the race,
And every morn they gathered at the mound,
For many after years, till they had grown
A nation strong in numbers, and had thrown
The seeds of generation far and wide,
And found the latent valleys without guide.
The lakes are made a tribute to their spoil,
And all the riches of the virgin soil
Were tested by those hardy argonauts of old ;
And though they sought no fleece of shining gold,
They penetrated all the wilderness
That lay unclaimed before them to possess.

God drops no nobler anchorage on earth,
Than those who mold a nation, and a name ;
Whose travail in the wilderness gives birth
To some great epoch, without thought of fame.
The pioneers of empire, for all time,
Are gold-dust, from the placers of our homes—
The surface croppings from a nation's prime,
The mellow acre of the richest loams.
They overgrow the boundaries of life,
And push the horizon far out in space.
With lethargy they wage a ceaseless strife,
And with the whirling earth, they keep their pace.
All honor to the soul who sets his stake
Where human kind have never trenched before ;
Where only God his thunders o'er it shake,
And solitude shall murmur, "nevermore."
Such men are sovereigns, though they grasp no crown,
And raise no jewelled scepter in the hand ;
Yet are they Princes, in their bronze and brown,
And demonstrate their fitness to command.

The Norsemen, on the North Atlantic wave ;
    Columbus, passing out in unknown seas ;
De Soto, gaining but an unknown grave ;
    The hardy Pilgrims, on their bended knees ;
The Argonauts, upon the Western slope—
    These are the souls no human praise can reach.
Each, in their turn, gave empire back to hope,

And all are greater than the gift of speech.
No pen can lustre their unfading claim ;
No cenotaph do honor to their dust—
These are crown jewels on the brow of Fame;
    Their conquest is supreme, their laurels ever just.

Yet, in the van of empire, still is left
    The noiseless print of ancestry more grand ;
Indentures chiseled in the highest cleft,
    By giants of a long forgotten land,—
The nameless graves of centuries untold ;
    The ashes of the prehistoric age ;
The self-forgetting litany of gold—
    How vast their monuments, how broad their page !
In what a grand democracy of death
    They lift their silent fingers to our years,
Melt our memorials with a single breath
    In mute companionship of life and tears !

We are but pygmies to the almighty past,
    The names we honor but the surface-mould ;
Beneath must lie an empire far more vast,
    Whose fundaments alone deserve the name of "old."

Not many years, till they had found the bed
    Of copper ore upon Superior's rim;
And hither many of the hardy ones were led
    By Orchas, quick in architrave, and fleet of limb ;

And many the fantastic implements he shaped
    For husbandry ; no want of theirs escaped
His eager scrutiny—the axe and blade,
    The rough-made pick, and the encumbered spade,
The vessels for the housewife, and the spear,
    And other weaponry for bison and for deer.
All these were fashioned in an uncouth way,
    And yet they filled the purpose of the day.

They had not reached the iron age of thought,
And what they made, necessity had taught ;
But riper years must ope the "Sampson Mine,"
And wake the rugged giant, in the shine
Of a meridian sunlight ; they little thought
Of what a Hercules remained unsought,
So near Missouri's border ; yet, not strange
Is their indicted ignorance—their range
Was circumscribed ; and iron was left to rest,
Till man had long been cradled on the breast
Of patient Mother Earth—not all at once
Did she give up her treasures ; and the dunce
Must grow into philosopher with years.
Experience with its battlehood of tears,
Is Nature's great interpreter ; we learn
But slowly, till the lessons fervid burn
Their impress into action ; then awakes
The slow-taught pupil into higher life—
Invention is the furnace-spark of strife ;

Necessity, the hand that wields the sledge
Upon the patient anvil of our needs,
And Providence makes good its wakeful pledge
With plenteous harvest ; from the dormant seeds
That lie unconed beneath our very feet
We stumble on to marvels, and awake
To find some giant force, in what we meet;
And in the insects of our path, leviathans, we greet.

Time's wheels, though shaken, never fail to track
The rut of empire, without turning back ;
They, ceaseless whirl, with lubricate of blood,
Drawn from a thousand channels on the way,
Unrusting, through the oxydizing flood,
To measure centuries, or mark a day.
And thus, the primal pioneers move on
To unaccustomed progress, on the banks
Of the confluent streams that scar the face
Of the great Western basin ; and their ranks
Are filled with happy husbandry ; the land
Gives back its tillage, with a lavish hand.

The forests and the streams were over-full
With fish, and flesh to feed them, and they pass
One conquest, to another, in the lull
Of untamed nature. Garnered as a mass
To fill their open hands, the native corn
Soon covered the rich valleys, and the plant,
So dalliant to the race, was early born.

Tobacco.   They were not adamant
Against the weaknesses so close allied
To human nature ; and there was excess,
And envy, emulence, and pride,
And all the ills that left their first impress ;
And yet God gave them peace.   No brother's hand
Was raised against a brother, and the years
Spread fruit and plenty over a fair land
Destined to futurehood of bitter, bitter tears.

DEPARTURE OF WABUN.

" Most governed is most wayward."   Very true ;
    Repeating history doth verify
That law from malefaction always grew,
    And with its ceasing, rulership must die,
    Except the common sway of Deity,
      When love and service shall together blend,
And man, from every earthly master free,
      Shall recognize his Father and his Friend.

These ancient prairie dwellers, had no need
Of stringent government ; a few to lead
In seeding and in harvest ; some to guide
In matters of religion, and of form ;
The rustic swain, and his compliant bride,
To join in wedlock ; and in time of storm,
To smooth the little intricates of life

With counsel, sage, and thus avoiding strife,
To guide their budding nation into bloom.
All claiming unction from the prophet's shade,
Still gave their worship to the god of day,
And their oblations on the altar laid.
Yet, the responsive accident of fire
Could never be recalled—they little knew
The secret of its coming ; and they shaped
No other pebbles like the one so true
To Uri's pleadings ; still they kept their faith
And reared their shapely mounds to meet the sun
With his first glance, and from the morning's breath
Retain their fervency, till day was done.
From out their number, some were set apart
For game and chase.   The buffalo and deer
And wild fowl, all, paid tribute to their skill,
And vale and forest echoed with their cheer.

But one of these, young Wabun, shunned the group,
And wandered by the forest streams alone.
Some called him "dreamer"; others tried to win
His mooding back to mirth ; but there was none
That seemed to reach the center of his soul ;
He joined not in the worship of his race,
And seemed to be so distant in his thought,
That one might search the Pleiad's in his face.

There shone a star upon the eastern rim—
 So suddenly it shot upon their view,

So brilliant and so placid, never dim
   Through storm and starlight, always lit anew.
They marveled much, and some were sore dismayed
   To seek the portents of this stranger star;
But not so, Wabun; he, all unafraid,
   Hailed it as answer from the dim afar,
And showed unwonted pleasure at its sight;
   His distance seemed to shorten, and his mind
Seemed mellowed by a new-born love to man—
   A quickened tenderness to help his kind.

"I wander in the forest; by the stream";
   (They gave earnest audience as he spake)
"And underneath the stars—and they all tell
The story of a great, forgotten God.
I listen to the murmuring of the rain,
And to the mighty thunder of the clouds;
And see the forked lightning, in its gleam,
Strike the great oak to shivers, in its path;
I see the maize upon a thousand fields;
I see the goodly carpet on the earth—
And every grassy thread a miracle—
I see the sun upon his track of light,
The moon upon her pathway in the sky—
And all do tell of this forgotten God.
For God is of the living, not the dead:
The tree, the sun, the moon, the stars, and all,
All fill their places; but are not alive

"As we, with thought, and purpose, and design ;
But each doth turn upon a steady crank
Held by a mighty and imperious hand.
The bison, and the deer, and all the birds,
Have life, and voice, and action, such as we ;
And yet they have no thought, except to live.
They build no houses, lay no harvests up—
We are their masters, with the right to kill.

"All things pay tribute to our prowent hands ;
All things we see are provident of us :
The sun to ripen, and the moon to watch,
The birds and flocks for us to gather flesh,
The forests and the prairies for our use,
The mines for metal, and the streams for fish—
All, all, pay tribute to our wasting hands.
Yet we are not a law unto ourselves :
Though masters, yet not gods, for we all die
And fall back into dust ; yet are we great,
And greatest of earth's creatures ; but for death,
We might claim highest unction ; but our power
Is limited ; wherefore, if we are highest type
Of creature earth, then must it surely be
That God is man, but of a higher mold;
Not subject unto death, but Lord of life.
And, if all earthly forces must conserve
Our being (highest born of all the earth),
Then back of us t he great Creator stands

" Unseen, as is Eternity unseen,
But felt, as is each ripple of her waves,
Upon the shores of our unstable life.
The greater is not seen. We do not see
The very thought that holds us in control.

    " Thus have I doled, and pondered on it well,
Until, upon my vision dawned that star;
And as upon some errand quickly sent
(I know not how I went, I felt so light),
I sped upon its rays, o'er vale, and hill,
And o'er a vaster water than the lakes—
A grand expanse of green and surging waves.
And, on, still on, till just before my face
A mother, and an infant at her breast,
And many seeming wise and stately men
Bending in homage and with offerings choice,
Of sweetly-scented vintage ; then I sought
To find the wherefore of this sweet emprize;
And I was told this was the Son of God—
The One that was to come, the mighty One,
Redeemer of the world ; that man had sinned
And he was come to set at one the race
With the All-Father ; that we had been made
In God's own image ; that the sun and moon
Were but his handiwork.   To Him alone
(Invisible, yet always looking on)

"Should homage be ascribed.   All this was short
Yet was it printed on my pliant breast,
And cannot be erased.   I seek no name
And claim no higher homage for the gleam
Vouchsafed my vision of the mighty past
And prescience of the future ; tis enough
To know my steps directed, and to feel
That in my darkness I have found out God.
No more the unknown God, but evermore
The ripened type of the diviner man ;
And as we reap the tokens of his love,
Remember him as Father Man of men—
The Infinite Perfection of our race."

Much more he said which made a deep impress
Upon the hardy hunters, and the less
Were those who gave no sanction to his word ;
The greater portion followed him in thought,
And soon in deed.   The votaries of the sun
Made most malignant onslaught, and they sought
To drive the thoughtful Wabun from his " dream."
The strife was vain.   They in their fervent hope
Turn to the East, into the wilderness—
The grand Druidic of the Eastern slope,
And, hid to all but God, they penetrate
The deep recessess of their broad estate.

The gentle Wabun held for many years
His hand upon the pulses of their thought ;

Sometimes upon their love, sometimes their fears,
His fervent purity, its impress wrought.
He led them to the thousand untold charms
That sparkle on the rugged Eastern slope.
He bared to them the great Creator's arms,
And, in God's grandest alphabet, he read their highest hope.

Niagara was but a giant scroll,
    Whereon God writ a token of his strength ;
The muttering voice of its unceasing roll
    Was but a cadence of the mighty length
That measures the eternities of life.
    Its grandeur but one glitter of the gold
That played upon his vesture ; that the strife
    Of waters was the stream so cold,
Down which humanity as rudely rushed ;
    Without a thought for their eternal good,
With all the semblance of the Father crushed,
    They pass down in the surge of death's unceasing
        flood.   .

The broad Atlantic lashing at the shore,
    Was human passion—with the balance gone ;
Endeafening the graces with its roar,
    And blindly lashing the Eternal throne.
Into these miniatures, God thrust himself,
    That every wave might glitter with his name,
That every rock might hold upon its shelf
    Some semblance that their reverence might claim.

The kindlier tokens of paternal care,
On Nature's face, were beaming everywhere.

And yet, how few of us, can truly blend
The creature with Creator, in our sight;
And from the Father, grasp the hand of friend,
Whose stars of providence outshine the night !
Our eyes are fettered with an earthly bound,
Our narrow horizon will not enlarge ;
Our gaze, star fixed, will drop back to the ground,
And will not with the infinite surcharge.
Only God's hand can push the barriers back,
And give our vision unimpeded range ;
And with each respite, on the weary track,
Fix the unchangeable, where all is change.

RETURN AND STRIFE.

No wonder, that when Wabun passed away,
Their torpid natures should have lost the charm
That held so perfect, with its gentle sway,
Yet slacked so quickly, with the palsied arm.
Infirmities are easy to impart,
And through the generations, they come down ;
But God must place his hand upon each heart,
And press each brow where he would drop a crown.

Long brotherhood of forest, storm and flood,
Had schooled them for the turbulence of life.

The wraith of Nature made them men of blood ;
  The war of elements, the ocean's strife,
The thunder of Niagara now heard,
  The lashing of Atlantic on the beach,
The slogan of the forest— in a word
  The carnival, at rife, within their reach,
All served to spur their natures into storm.
  How many catch the key-note of their song
From the surrounding elements, and warm
  Their frozen energies, and make them strong
In earth's unceasing alchemy !   Much more
  The untutored savage ; he has lost the key,
And must from Nature's chalice find the door,
  Through which to penetrate life's mystery.

And many generations passed away,
  Since these stern foresters had dwelt apart
From their ancestral brethren ; till the day
  When in their higher prowess, from the heart
Of the great forest fastnesses, they spring
  As panthers, on their unsuspecting prey.
They have grown strong in weaponry, yet cling
  To Deity, in their untutored way.
The "happy hunting ground " to them is Heaven ;
  And the "Great Spirit " still to them is God ;
Yet, from their hearts, all tender passions driven,
  They smite their brethren with a heavy rod.

A long and ceaseless struggle, many years,
Alternately, invasion and defense,
Till they are driven southward ; and the fears,
That Kohen's prophecy would be fullfilled
And back of this, the agony intense
Of impotence in prayer so deeply chilled
The hearts of these poor children of the sun,
That they gave easy conquest to their foes ;
And thus the struggle stubbornly begun,
So unresisting now, was finished without blows.

When man is shorn of strength, and there is left
Only Ominpotence, we kiss the rod—
The very rod that smites us.   In the cleft
We would attempt to hide from Deity;
Yet in his anger is an answered prayer—
The consciousness of presence; though we flee,
The wrath of love, is proof of constant care.
But when we beat against the empty air,
And every echo sends us back dispair,
And even superstition, fails to foil
Our souls with the deceptive glow of spoil,
Then are we bittered, and our path made black ;
We grope in mists, Cimmerian, on the wrack
Of constant and interminable doubt,
A natural prey, and easy put to rout.

To South, and West, they turn their fateful way
Beyond the Mississippi ; and their day

Seemed lighted with a new influx of hope.
 The sun embraced them with a warmer smile;
The mellow fragrance of the Southern slope
  Added entrancement each succeeding mile.
Not all at once the exodus took place,
  For they were many, and had scattered wide;
Yet to the southward all had set their face
  To seek in other fields a place to hide
From cruel persecutions. When our kin
  Lends its consanguined arder to the dart,
How more intent, with vengeful purposes,
  How heavier is the load upon the heart !

They scatter into fragmentary clans,
  And in the earnest of their added woe,
Give birth to new religious phantasies.
  The unclogged streams of superstition flow,
When down the mountains, and across the moors,
  The heavy, swollen torrents sweep along,
Throwing their scattered wrecks upon the shores,
  And breaking barriers, however strong.
Baal was great, when Baalbec reared her crest
  And column after column gave her grace
And all the East upon her beauty smiled ;
  But when the "owls and bats" usurped her place,
The god had fallen. In the temple dust,
Where man, with his immortal, had so strove
To make the marble animate (in vain,

Like other myriad phantoms of the brain)
Time fashions into ghostly hands, that sternly point
  above.
And so, God reaps involuntary praise,
  From every fashioning of man's design ;
His ways, indeed, cannot be called our ways ;
  Yet his hozannas, from each crumbling shrine,
Teach us the servitude of all the past;
  That human hands but fashion Heavenly aids ;
  That every sculptured mythmark only fades
Into eternal sunshine, at the last.

  Some crossed the mountain ramparts of the West ;
Some lingered still upon the Eastern slope ;
  The empire yet was open to their zest,
And all were buoyant with a new-born hope.
  But war, like pestilence, doth warp our lives,
And like contagion, it infects the air.
  Peace comes in measure, but it never thrives
Directly after conflict, till grows fair
  The flesh so lately scarred.   Intestine war
Made ravage of their ranks ; they ill could spare
  Their bravest, yet the first to fall in fraticidal jar.
The lines, by conflict, soon were closely drawn,
And from the night of struggle nations dawn,
Whose chiefs assume the King's prerogative.
Clans fall, and clansmen perish ; nations live
That pass chaotic conflict, and ensphere

Their crude material, as a new-born world,
To individual phalanxes, and rear
Their rude escutcheon.   As in ether whirled,
The new born planet tracks its trial course ;
   So must this human query find its way,
And failure is its fashion; but still worse
   Are those who fail to grapple with the day,
But look supinely on while vested rights
   Are trampled under foot, and raise no hand
In deprecating gesture; from the heights
   Of grim impartial history will stand
Unfading letters, written to the shame
   Of those whose scourges fail to make a name.

PREHISTORIC RENDEZVOUS OF THE AZTECS.

On either side the crest of the Madre,
Where mountains kiss their hands to either sea,
One slope to blush upon the opening day,
   The other, to drop down its tapestry
And hold the hand for promise of return,
Three nations, as three stars, to being burn.
The Toltecs, purest of the primal race,
The Chichamecs, devoted to the chase,
And Aztecs, strongest in the arts of war—
All, seeming thrown beneath one fateful star.
No painter limnes upon his labored scroll,
   Be it fantastic, feast, or forest shades,

As war upon its victims ; from the soul
(Plastic as new damped clay) it never fades
Till Time has ironed out the furrowed past;
And Peace, by laying fevered brows to rest,
. Over the present has its mantle cast ;
Then Nature folds its wardling to its breast.
So on these nations had been writ, in brief,
The deep-burned liturgy of hardened strife,
And through the furnace of their pungent grief,
They learn to plant the rootlets of their life.
One thing is never lacking, at the time,
When in their nascent passions, nations rise:
The craft of Priests, in every age and clime,
To " point a moral," or portend the skies.
And so, from cast-off altars to the sun,
New pleadings to new conjured gods arose ;
The selfish passions since the world begun,
All seek supernal outlet on their foes.

One thing, not far from truth, grew into form :
The thought of one great, universal heart,
That beat against the window pane of thought,
And formed of all existences a part.
How near the passions of mankind will verge,
Sometimes, upon the borderland of bliss !
And all the race is bettered if they urge
Continuous march ; nor turn their steps amiss;
A little light would lead them on to God,

And lacking, it the race for ages plod.
O that the infant eye of every race
  Might recognize at once the Master's face!
All brought their tribue to Tonatiuh's shrine,
Still burnishing the sun with rays divine.
True worship strengthens in the wake of years ;
  Its song grows rhythmal with repeated chant ;
Its beauty lingers, though it disappears ;
  Rekindle, and it melts the adamant.
But worship on a purely human base,
  Though it may work its legends into song
And deify the noblest of its race,
  Can never be unquestionably strong.
The happenings of Nature clog its wheels ;
  The elements brush down its cobweb foils;
And from its mimicry the heart appeals,
  And heavenly souls are not for human toils.
It is impossible to still the brain
  By merely human fiat at it thrust ;
Man journeys out, and he returns again—
  The Father's voice alone can call him from the dust.

And yet, each effort of the human soul,
To force existence for its latent wings,
Is of an energy that leaps control,
Whose germ from our immortal nature springs.
The very latch-key of the eternal realm,
Though touched in ignorance, commands the door.

A more than human wisdom guides the helm,
As we approach the palm-extending shore.
The hungry arms that reach out after God,
Are as the infants for the parent's breast ;
The soul is weary of its fruitless plod,
And Nature beckons it to perfect rest.
What though the stream be poisoned, if its flow
   Seeks only the great ocean to be lost ;
   Not long upon its bosom is it tossed,
Ere it recovers its old healthful glow.
The old-time sparkle of the mountain spring,
   Gleams in the dew-drop that returns to earth.
   No poison lurks within the second birth,
It ever carries healing on its wing.
Thus, howsoe'er the soul may find its way,
   Over the wilderness to Jordan's plain,
   It shall not fail of its eternal gain,
The night so trackless shall break into day.
The saint, whom angels ushered through the gate,
   With pæans of rejoicing, once did grope
   And lose his way, and loose his hold on hope —
No soul that reaches it is told to wait.
God waits upon the effort to reply,
   And seeing human hands stretch out for aid,
   His stronger palm is soon upon them laid—
Our weakness is the signet he cannot deny.

THE TOLTECS JOURNEY SOUTH.

The Toltecs were the first to break the way
  Toward the vertex of the Summer sun ;
To catch the fervor of his ripest ray,
  And talismise the pilgrimage begun.
And after many days their fasting eyes
  Are feasted with Mexitli's* lovely plain—
So like a newly-fashioned paradise,
  An almost Eden, sprung to life again.
Her placid lakes gave back her deep blue sky
  In rivalry of Nature—Nature's charms
Do cast reflected multiples, and try
  To fold us in with her unnumbered arms.
Not all we see, but all we feel, invites,
  Together with our seeing, to secure
An unrestricted homage ; all unite
  In this uncovered world, so rich and pure
And lade with sunshine, ripened into form,
  Concentered rays to leaves and blossoms grown,
The larch impendent with its verdant cone,
  The oak's historic battlement of storm,
The cypress mourning and exultant palms.
  The provident maguey, whose offered alms
Found ready acceptation at their hands,
  The maize, which they had known in northern lands,

Mexitli, Toltec for Mexico, also the god of war.

Were native to her rich and virgin soil
And gave the husbandman unstinted spoil.

And thus, with Nature and themselves at rest,
Fresh inspiration from the God of peace
Expands and energizes every breast,
And fettered manhood labors for release.
Invention is emanciapation ; Time
Doth loosen Nature's fetters ; man invents
Not one of those discoveries sublime
    That couples his poor name with consequence.
The world had moved a million years or so
    Ere Galileo blundered into prison
For telling how we are compelled to go.
    The fog of superstition had not risen ;
And he whose brain peered up above the cloud,
    To widen the horizon of his thought,
Must be content to leave the gnarlish crowd
    Of puppets and of priestcraft who have fought
The van of progress, immemorial time,
    In fear some newly loosened truth might break
Some preconcerted dogma, deeming crime
    The impulsive movement of the soul to slake
The thirst that God implanted there, to burn
    Its way into the hidden and unseen,
And find new thoroughfares for its return,
    And on creation's outer verge new entities to glean.

So did these primal pioneers look out
   Beyond the compass of their husbandry,
And challenge their surroundings ; manly, stout,
   And earnest did they seek the mystic tree
Of knowledge in this Eden of the West,
   Not interdicted by Divine decree,
But always open to the manly quest
   And the unflagging purpose to be free.
The zodiac gave up its lettered scroll
   To their inquiries ; and the measured year
Unsealed the clasp that held it from control,
   And truths that had seemed very far, revealed them-
      selves quite near.

Their rudely fashioned lodges soon gave way
   To buildings of a more pretentious form ;
The forests and the quarries and the clay
   Were forced to human vassalage.   The charm
That held the forest templary from spoil
   Was not entirely broken ; after years
And Christian conquest must consume the toil
   And travail of the centuries.   Our tears,
Are but a poor atonement for the brand
   Our westward march has made on Nature's back.
We mourn our forest fastnesses too late ;
   With hand unbridled we have torn their face,
And given legal sanction to their fate—
   But what companionship can take their place?

Nearest to Nature's very heart of hearts,
  The verdant monarchs beckon us to God;
Their benison with life alone departs ;
  They testify of Eden from the sod.
O man ! that thy perfection should be lost,
  When so much pefectness is left on earth !
How much of bitterness ! With what a cost
    Didst thou forget the sacred touch that hallowed thee
    at birth !

The worship of Hurakin, " Heart of Heaven,"
  Spoke of a healthier, higher growth of soul,
The consciousness of sins to be forgiven ;
  A god, whom weakness could at once control ;
A prophecy, of Fatherhood to come ;
  A ray that pencils from the " great white throne ; "
A voice to energies, that had been dumb
  For many centuries—prophetic groan
Of man's insatiate thirst for betterment,
  Not all in vain.   The white-winged dove of peace
For many years was theirs ; they came and went
  Beyond their borders, without let or lease ;
Found sunnier climes to South ; and, as a charm
  Was laid upon their footsteps, they advance
To hover closer to their ancient god.
  They still were pliant to his fateful glance,
And scanned his burnished surface to inquire
  His potency in human destiny.

They had forgot the legend of his fire,
　　Yet, from his searching, steadfast eye, not one of
　　them were free.

So pass they out from the historic ken—
　　Theirs, no aggressive way-mark on the earth.
We linger on their passage, and the pen
　　Would gladly pour regret upon the dearth
Of the indentures they have left to mark
　　Their peaceful, noiseless tread upon the shore ;
But it is vain ; yet out of all this dark,
　　One lesson may we glean : That evermore
The souls that move with nature on her march
　　Are those who drop, as she drops down her leaves ;
They fill the earth with fruitfulness, and arch
　　The highway of the nations with their sheaves ;
They sleep to history, but wake to God ;
　　Theirs is the pass-key through eternal gates ;
They write no vengeful Sanscrit on the sod ;
　　They linger at no earthly court, but the recording ser-
　　aph waits
To write them blessed of the Lord, the jewels of the
　　fates.

THE AZTECS—AZTLAN.

The silver current of the upper Grande,
　　And where the Gila penetrates the East,

The Zuni lines its rocky bed with sand,
  New ground from granite that has been released
From mountain base. The vertebrate Madre
  Breaks into several center-stays of spine,
Which form the watershed that feeds the sea,
  On either side the sunny slopes recline.
Where Coronado laid in after years
  The scepter of his Sovereign, and bespoke
The unbroke silence, as the cycle nears
  The bending of the neck to Hispagniola's yoke.

Here was the fabled Aztlan ; and the race,
  Whose ancestry had circled half the globe,
Have now their latest destiny to face.
  O ! could they peer the darkness through, and probe
The deep recesses of impending time !
  Look for one moment on what was to be !
How would they cling to this rude mountain clime,
And bar the door of their futurity !

The Aztecs were a proud and prowent race ;
In the dispersal at the far Northeast,
Now many years, they held the leading place ;
Yet, in their husbandry, they were the least.
Their hands were skilled to turbulence and strife ;
The bow, the lance, and the rude hunter's knife—
Such were their ready implements ; but peace
Found them all unacquainted ; her surcease
Requires a range of weaponry diverse.

The hands that hew down others, lips that curse,
Both must be newly christened; and the arts
That unify the race with nature's ways
Must hard their hands and reimburse their hearts,
And time their lips with sunnier kinds of lays.

As if to fill the interim, there grew
From their own ranks, the fittest kind of guide,
A pastoral leader; who by instinct knew
The flowery paths that lead on either side
The verdant fields of husbandry and thrift;
The worthy Moctheuzoma* had this gift,
And led them to the conquest of the soil—
That easy conquering that seeks its spoil
Only where God intended it for man,
The fruits of his own labor. Thus began
An era of self-discipline, that led
The Aztecs on to greatness; and that shed
A tender halo over after years,
When memory will mingle with our tears.

He turned their eyes upon the talcite ledge,
And said: "Behold, this is Tonatuah's pledge
Of providence against the Summer's heat
And the cold frosts of Winter; quarry it,
And fashion it for framework to your homes.
For centuries it has withstood the storm,

---

*Moctheuzoma, the original Aztec name for Montezuma, commonly spoken of as the Elder Montezuma, a pastoral leader still remembered in their legends.

"To wait upon your coming ; let your feet
Be busy with its treasures."   Then he turned
To where the clay, for years, had been inurned,
And said :   " Make use of this ; 'tis Thaloc's* gift.
The mighty thunderer hath torn it down,
And ground it into ashes, for your use ;
Mold it in shapely fragments, and the sun,
The warm-faced Tonatuah, will pour out
His warmest rays to bake it back to stone.
And more, this pliant clay has aptitudes
For vessels of all kinds, and yours are rude ;
So in a hundred ways you may improve."

Then, pointing to the forest, thus he spoke :
" There Tonatu' and Thaloc both did shake
Their well-filled branches to the earth for us,
That we might gather fruit, for any taste.
These noble trees have swelled the turf for years,
And now will bend the neck for our support.
We must be provident ; for they do point
Their myriad fingers to the hands that gave,
Mute monitors, to beckon us of Heaven.

" The fish and fowl, and all the vast menage
That track our mountain slopes, are all our own.
But look out on the earth, whose grassy turf
Lifts up its thousand homages to Heaven ;

---

*Thaloc, the Aztec god of the lightning.

" Whence must we gather fruit of our own toil.
The maize will grow if planted ; the legume
Will ripen ; and our hands will surely fill,
If we but ask the earth and gods to help
And second our endeavors.   We must work.
The river, from the mountain, rushes on ;
The mountain shakes its thousand plumes at her ;
The stars do not keep quiet in the skies ;
All nature is alert and on the watch ;
And man must bear his burden at the mill."

Thus, did he lead them to their better selves,
 And ravel out the intricates of life
In wisdom's stern and simple litany ;
 Gave trenchent lessons to the man and wife,
And scattered homes upon new harvest fields.
 And he, who sets a household altar up,
And sanctifies it with the name of home,
 Fresh sprinkled from the sacred nuptial cup,
Is Heaven's Ambassador in human form.
 The hearthstone is the herald of advance ;
The hanging of each homely crane, like one
 Of God's unnumbered irridescent plants,
Sheds rainbow hues on all it shines upon,
 And blessings bend each limb upon its tree.
Thrice happy is the nation thus begun,
 ·For it has found the track of destiny.

The mines he opened, and laid bare the beds
Of precious minerals that underlie
The bases of our mountain chains.
" For all our wants, we have a full supply,"
Thus spake the seer. "We shall not beat in vain
Against the bars that keep our souls from flight.
Our birth is built around by providence ;
Our wants are wickets to unmeasured wealth.
If we but find the turnstile to the field,
We have but half the hill of life to climb ;
The other half fades out as we advance;
When we have toiled out half-way distance up,
Lo! we have found the summit, and descend.

" Thus do we work together with the gods ;
If we but do our best, it is enough ;
When we put out our arms, they reach to us,
Though they do span the universe, to meet
And draw us up, the shining heights of life.
So in our daily plodding ; if we sow,
The gods will furnish harvest ; if we build,
The gods have made the quarry and the clay ;
Whatever purposes we have in life,
If they be only for our betterment,
The crude material is at our hands ;
We only fashion it to suit our wants;
Nor is the measure stinted to our needs,
But all our vessels fill to overflow.

" Look over the green fields ! Great is our want,
But greater the supply ; on every hand
The wild flowers lift their heads, and what are these
But kisses thrown from Heaven to win us back?
Our appetites are but our weaker parts,
And easy satisfied ; not so our souls ;
They have external longings to supply ;
And all that beautifies and brightens earth
Are forecasts of a kingdom yet to come.
As on earth's surface may be found the flowers,
So, underneath the shining metals are
The surplus of a generous providence.
Our fathers, on the borders of the lakes,
Did fashion implements of husbandry
From inexhaustive mines ; but here we have
In lesser quantities, much brighter ores,
Fit mostly for adornment and exchange.

" Man is not satisfied with 'hand to mouth.'
The beasts roam through the forests and are filled,
And therewith are content ; not so with man.
Two worlds break on his vision ; and the one
Must interlock the other in his life,
Or he goes blindly out into the night.
And it is well earth gives no perfect rest,
Or the hereafter would fall out of sight.
Man is the one ambitious animal
Who seeks for empire, as the brute seeks food ;

The tame necessities are not enough,
But all the precious under flowers of earth
Must fill the measure of his discontent.
All men are not alike, and some must hold
The fullest measure of life's luxuries ;
These pay their surplus for the others' toil ;
With them the shining metals will be held
As medium for barter and for trade.
And as Earth decks her bosom with the flowers,
So will the human race adorn themselves
And blossom out with variance of gems."

Though, still encumbered with their ancient myths,
    He pointed out the harmony of Heaven ;
Gave why and wherefore to the dread eclipse.
    Not his to tell them how the earth is driven
Upon its swinging orbit over space ;
    And yet he measured out the perfect year ;
He looked stern Nature bravely in the face,
    And seemed to question her without a fear.
Transcendent genius ; thus to grapple Truth
    Across the path still covered from his sight,
Yet is she merciful ; her name is Ruth ;
    She never perches on so grand a height,
But she will answer to her children's call,
    And spread her wings to fly to their embrace—
This link was never broken by our fall,
    And writes Evangel on our troubled race.

With his own hand he led them to the field,
With his own hand he taught them how to build ;
He showed them what true husbandry would yield,
How all their empty measures could be filled
By wakeful industry.   "Well pointed toil
Is touchstone to earth's treasure-box," said he.
"Our fathers may enrich us with their spoil,
And we may thus evade the beaten path ;
Yet, lying dormant on our fathers' beds,
Our waste brings want upon our children's heads.
Far better that each hand be labor-marked,
That all may know the purchase of their lives ;
He loses half the journey who goes out
To the incertitudes of other worlds,
Who has not tasted what his hands have won
On this, his trial sphere."

Thus in well-chosen words, and earnest deeds,
He planted fruit that crowded out the weeds.
Ruled by divinest right of master-mind,
By wisdom and humility combined,
By heart, as well as head and hand, he wrought ;
For there be many who can ne'er be taught
By any else than throbbing 'gainst their own,
Of some great royal heart; this is their throne ;
And he who sways in scepterhood of love,
Gets his vicegerent from the throne above.
Through many years did Moctheuzoma reign ;

And Aztlan prospered, and the race grew strong;
And when his body passed to earth again,
His spirit, with its wisdom, lingered long.

Thus, with a twilight halo pass the great
    Across the threshold with a noiseless tread ;
We linger but a moment at the gate
    To pay our homage to the honored dead ;
Then turn to find them still inurned with us.
    Their silence is more eloquent than words,
Their passing out is but life's overplus,
    Their tongues are tempered into two-edged swords.
They speak across the chasm of their graves,
    In weightier words, in thoughts far more intense ;
In life they mingled with its thousand waves—
    It is God's way ; death ripens eloquence.

Time trolls along with its unceasing march,
    And Aztlan has outgrown her former bounds ;
She holds the center of the ancient arch,
    On the historic ladder's highest rounds.
She sways the queenly scepter of the past
Above the waymarks of a hundred realms ;
Yet leaves but hints of the grand overcast,
Through which she burns her way, and overwhelms
Our thoughts with all the possibles of time.
We can but poorly comprehend, yet write her most sub-
    lime.

PART THIRD.

ANAHUAC.*

THE AZTEC'S JOURNEY AND SETTLEMENT SOUTH.

Another turn of fortune's fickle wheel.
They journey to the South, and cast their lot
Upon Mexitli's lovely plain ; the heel
    Of other nations has forestalled the spot,
And they must win their way through turbulence
    To reach the border of the placid lake,
Where conquest waits their hardly purchased chance ;
    And all of Anahuac shall feel the shake
Of their unconquered tread.   Not many years
    Ere nation follows nation to their thrall ;
And many are the hot, convulsive tears,
    Through which we read of any people's fall.
Our homes and hearthstones are so near the same,
Or column-capped, or made of homely clay—
    Marble and gold can make no higher claim
    Than thatch or brushwood, so they bear the name
Of household, hallowed for centuries or held but for a
    day.
As if to track a thousand similes

---

* Anahuac, the country dominated by the Aztecs at the time of the conquest.

Of thorn and rose, of laughter and of tears,
War strikes its hand upon all sacristies ;
(Religion must be bent to its decrees)
Holding our destinies—our hopes and fears
Are all within its baleful balance thrown.
It beats upon the organ of our lives, and history repeats
    the wild, discordant moan.
So nations, whose lost anchorage must pay
The penalty of their forgetfulness,
Seek out phantasmal deities to prey
Upon their vitals in their sore distress.

    Mars, or Mexitli* : though the one be crowned
With all the glory that bedecks old Rome,
The idols of the other, fiercely ground
To powdered pulp by Spain's invading host.
How much of agony they both have cost
Ask of the millions lost to life and home !
Ambition makes a Cæsar : it is well
    It gives some recompense for all its crime ;
For it has made the earth an endless hell,
    Crowding its woes upon the lap of time—
And yet, religion spurs it to the test,
    And priests have been the primates of its throne,
Chanting their auguries to fire its breast,
    Braying all history with their undertone.

---

* " Mars or Mexitli." I have taken the easier of the names given to the war-
god. Huitzilopotchli or Mexitli both were used, the former more in general use
than the latter, at the time of the conquest.

Nor is the "manger," with its cradled Christ,
　　Free from the misinterpreting of Priest.
　The cross where God and man have kept their tryst,
Been changed to leaven for inglorious feast—
　God! must future draw its cadence from the past,
And plow its furrow through the same red mould?
　Must nations be in the same furnace cast,
And man, the master, bought, and scourged, and sold?
Then is creation but a lie accursed,
And better that the doom upon it burst .
No.　Though experience may slowly turn,
And man may learn as slowy, yet we learn.
The risen Christ did break the grasp of death,
And empire, dead in trespasses, will yet receive its breath.

Aztlan must pass through all the fated field
　Of mythologic peculence and lore,
And to their sturdy priestcraft blindly yield,
　.To cipher out the destinies in store.
They must propitiate the gods with blood,
　Especially their war-god must be fed,
And to supply their deities with food
　Their fated subjects must be freely bled.
So superstition whets the fatal blade,
　Which culminates in human sacrifice.
The maw of Huitzilopotchli* must be stayed,
　And altars with their thousand victims rise.

————
　Huit-zilo-potch-li, the Aztec war-god.

Sad proof of imperfection in the race,
  Nay, more, the very demon in the breast;
Their ignorance alone is plea for grace,
  When in their filthiness they stand confessed.
"Ye must be born again," the Savior said;
  And history, through time, has craved this birth.
Man and his Maker must indeed be wed,
  If we would bring redemption to the earth.
The empty riddle of the crucifix,
  The shallow rattle of the Christian creeds,
Will leaven nothing if we fail to mix
  The ripened grain of soul-inspiring deeds.
The past accuses us with bony hands;
  We cannot shun its cold and cruel eyes;
The glass is turning with our future sands—
  We face eternal destinies. God grant we be more
    wise!

THE EMPIRE OF MONTEZUMA.

The Star looked down at the Mountain;
  And the Mountain looked down at the Sea;
And there was no malice in either one's breast,
  Each was called by the Deity
To fill its place in the region of space
  Of the fathomless Yet-to-be.
The Star didn't fall on the Mountain,
  Nor the Mountain smite the sea;
But each gave cheer in the other's ear,

And they dwelt in harmony.
Why didn't the Mountain say to the Star :
  " Begone, with your impudent stare !"
Or the Sea to the Mountain : " How dare you intrude,
  You presumptuous imp of the air?"
Why didn't they ? they were not human ;
  They couldn't talk, as we talk;
They were not born of a woman;
  They never had learned to walk.

They had learned the language of patience ;
  They had learned to bear, and be dumb ;
They had learned to hold, through heat and cold,
  Their load, till the Master should come.
O infinite language of silence !
  O eloquent, voiceless speech !
Help us to bear the ills that are,
  And fetter us each to each,
Till all our envy goes out with the Sea,
  And our malice goes out with the star,
And we silently bear what is to be —
  Like the Mountain—gazing afar
To the infinite depths of an endless world,
  Where eternity spreads its zone,
Where planets, countless as grains of sand,
  Gaze out on the " great white throne."

The pale-faced prophet Quetzalcoatl*
Had gone to the rising sun ;
In his wizard boat he was seen to float,
To where the day was begun,
Without a sail on the wings of the gale,
For the land of Tlappalan†
He waved back his followers from the sea,
Saying he would certainly come again,
In the golden future, yet to be,
And the gods should dwell on the earth as men.
They had made him a god, because he was good—
Not always the case in the mystic love—
They had carved his image in stone and wood,
And his shrines were built on the pyramid's floor.
They called him the god of the earth and air,
And his legends were many, and often told;
And the priests, with sacrifice and prayer,
Reaped a heavy harvest of fruit and gold.
And oft were their faces turned to the East,
To claim *his* promise, who *was* to come;
And they watched the surge of the gulf's green yeast,
And yet the years had continued dumb.

———

*Quetzalcoatl, the god of the harvest, probably some ancient leader deified. See Prescott.

†Tlappalan, the Elysian to which Quetzalcoatl passed, probably referred to the chambers of the sun.

Nezahualcoyotl sleeps with his fathers,*
  And his son now reigns in his stead;
His *goodness* succeeds to the living,
  But his *wisdom* goes out with the dead,
For both in the Lord of Tezcuco
  Had been richly and happily wed.
Two nations, strike hands o'er the waters,
  Tezcuco and Aztlan are one,
By the league that their fathers had plighted,
  Since they entered this land of the sun.
So, the King of their neighbor, Tezcuco,
  Has come to the Aztec Court,
To assist them in crowning the Monarch,
  A Prince of much goodly report.
He is found on the steps of the temple ;
  He has served, both as warrior and Priest ;
He has brought many victims to slaughter—
  The realm has been greatly increased
By the sturdy sway of his conquering arm.
  And now, he is called to reign,
The last of his race, to fill the place,
  Whose honor shall prove but a life-long pain.

Montezuma† was young, but his sword was old,
And the war-god was glutted with victims and gold.

'Nez-a-hual-co-yotl, one of the famous kings of Tezcuco (a nation allied to that
of the Aztecs). Prescott enlarges on his character, truly a wonderful one for the
time and age.
  †Montezuma, a corruption from the original Aztec, which was Moctheuzoma.

A pledge of his prowess : a promise to fate,
That the nation would prosper, the King prove great.
Some men are great in sorrow—there be tears
That crystalize to diamonds at the last.
They need the weight of carbonizing years ;
Yet, how they glitter after these have past!
Life needs the tempering at such a forge,
Or it would brittle at the lightest touch ;
But when the burden is but one vast gorge,
The weary soul must cry, " It is too much."

Nezahualpilli* places the crown on his head,
And the victims bleed, and the altars burn ;
The words of admonishment all are said,
And the buoyant crowd to their homes return.
"'The King is dead !" "Long live the King !"
" Hail !" and "farewell !" how closely tread
The steps of the living upon the dead !
How are both touched with a single spring !
Nezahualpilli soon passes away,
And the rival King, he so lately crowned,
Divides his Kingdom, and makes a prey,
A figment, with empire's empty sound.
And Montezuma outleaps the King ;
But is lord of an empire reaching the sea ;
And many nations their tribute bring,

---

*Nez-a-hual-pil-li, successor to Neza-hual-co-yotl, and a worthy one, though
not so gifted.

And some of the weak to the southward flee,
To pass the reach of his powerful arm,
And lift new prodigies to the sky,
To meet Earth's sunshine, shadow, and storm,
To finish the race, to falter and die.

He gathers his treasures from myriad mines.
The cotton and aloe are wove into cloth.
The banana and maize and wild forest vines,
While they load to repletion, are proof against sloth.
His palace is burnished with every hue
    Of the rainbow tints of his fabulous land,
    Where Nature entravails on every hand
To bring new beauties of life to view.
There are drapes of feather-cloth deftly made,
There were plumes and plushes of richest craft,
There were broidered robes where the colors played,
Like the hands that made them, dainty and daft.
His harem equaled his Ottoman peer,
    There was beauty of every hue and mold—
    The shy and the gay, the demure and bold—
That his provinces furnished from far and near.
    As fine a collection of beauty and grace,
    Of the flashing eye and the beaming face,
As is seen on the gates of the Euxine sea
At the present day, where the "powers that be,"
    With the Union Jack floating above the rest,
    Secures to that ill-omened bird its nest.

Their Teocallas* rose on every hand,
And half a hundred gods their worship claim ;
Their priestcraft is a strong and haughty band ;
Their Beckets and their Woolseys are the same
As those that cling upon the neck of time
Through all the feudal ages ; we may choose
The leeches of the Christian Church as best—
They sucked the blood the State could not refuse,
And so did these bedizzened, of the West.
These led their victims to the altars black,
Those wasted theirs by torturing and pain,
The fatal " itztli," gave the parting shock
To Aztec's victims ; but a blacker stain
Rests on thy skirts, thou bloody-mantled Spain !
Thou the avenger of a human wrong?
As well might Lucifer enrobe as saint,
An earthquake key the carol of a song,
Or old Caligula† bring a complaint !
" They slew their thousands ! " yes ; and what did'st thou ?
Thy thousands in the shadow of the cross ;
They took not on their perjured lips thy vow ;
Thy gold they did not mingle with their dross.
Through all the dark of ages did they grope ;
Through all the light of empire did'st thou graze ;
They pinioned superstition to their hope ;
The monody of hell was mingled with thy praise.

---

*Tecollas, Temples of worship.
†Caligula, a Roman Emperor whose name has become a synonym of crime.

Go back ! and scour the oxyd from the gem
   Thy lips have turned to ebony, and paint
Humiliation on thy doorsteps. Stem !
   Stem the black pool of Styx ! and find a saint
Whose blood shall gain forgiveness for thy past ;
   But count no beads upon the path of time—
Earth's execration is too justly cast—
   Thy very name, a synonym of crime !

They had their courts where justice was dispensed
   With what would shame the Janus-faced machine
We call our jurisprudence. They commenced
   What Christian polity was left to glean,
To her advantage in the after time.
   We write " anathema" above the gates
Of what we choose to call "barbaric clime ;"
   And yet, the blinded goddess often waits
To gather wisdom at *her* bare, black feet
   Which, bruised and blistered, tread the narrow way
To where the graces uninspired meet
   And superstition's night breaks into day.

They held the bond of family and home
   As firmly as more favored nations hold;
Their homes were castles, where no man could come
   Without the potent ses-a-me of gold.
The wealthy pluralized the name of wife
   (As many Bible patriarchs once did),

Their virtue was the average of life—
There were excrescences not easy hid.
Yet woman was more near her half of earth
Than she had reached in most of Christendom.
She held her value and could claim her worth;
Not bartered with the readiness of some
Self-styled enlightened.   Much is to be learned
In corners of the earth that we call "dark,"
Where jewels are for centuries inurned
That torches of enlightenment may tarnish with a spark.

We lay rude hands on temples not our own,
Nor little heed the human souls enshrined;
The sacred crevice of each hard-marked stone
But coldly cover with the virdict, "blind."
God help us, that we point a hand more pure,
And raise the casement with a grander trust ;
The hands that lift it must indeed be clean,
Or comes the humbling challenge, "Is it just?"
One "great white throne" shall judge us, one and all ;
One great white Hand shall hold the scales of fate,
Or clothed in light, or covered with a pall,
We tread the way through one eternal gate.
God grant the temples we so rudely spoil,
May not accuse us when we stand alone !
But hearts are human things, and they do coil
The infinite in blindness.   Not a groan
Escapes the index of the Father Son.

A child in blindness still is but a child,
And held with greater yearning to be won.
Our cold, hard hands cannot be reconciled
To one warm Heart that throbs for all mankind,
And covers, with a common love, the race;
And leads, with greater tenderness, the blind,
That they more closely feel His clasp, who cannot see
His face.

The arts of husbandry were well advanced:
They sowed and reaped unstinted from the soil;
The sun, with ripening fervor, on them glanced,
And gave them back, a hundred fold, their toil.
They had not lost their ancient faith in him,
Though other gods their scattered homage claim
His breast was their Elysian; never dim
The ancient hope that hung upon his name.
Their maize and maguey shone upon the plain,
Their chocolate gave nourishment and zest,
The corn gave recompense for sugar-cane,
Their banquets were provided with the best;
Fish from the ocean, fruits from every clime,
So diverse, yet within such easy reach;
The tropics and the temperates enchime
With all their plumaged babblings of speech;
And they interpreted the varied whims
That Nature holds embryoed in her breast.
They climbed the boughs and shook her heaviest limbs,

Too burdened for the garner to be missed.
This ancient mother never yet has failed
    Her children in their earnest search for food ;
She may be panoplied and heavy mailed,
    Yet does her larder furnish all when fully understood.

Take all in all, and measure by the test—
    The stern, hard test of history—and we find
That Aztlan, very far from being best,
    Still was a prodigy.   That she was blind
In her religious ethics, none deny ;
    That she had faults, no champion gainsays ;
She lifted bloody hands against the sky;
    She filled the avenging measure of her days.
But God is God, and man is always man ;
    And earthly judgment is at best a snare.
And never, since the human race began,
    Has turned to Heaven more piteous despair
Than her sad eyes, burnt out with agony ;
    Moaning above her nation, and her name,
The bitter monody of " Not to be,"
    The deep humiliation, and the shame
That sent her crouching at the foot of Spain ;
    (The fairest daughter of the wilderness)
Without a hand to solace in her pain,
    Or ray of hope to lighten her distress.

Could she been gently led, and tenderly,
    To higher life and holier resolve,

Had charity bent forth her noble sway,
  The Christian graces that with Earth revolve
Without the wasting friction, paid their suit
  To win her back to wakefulness from sin—
How would she compensate the victor's hand,
  And kiss the rod that smote with its regard!
But to be "drawn and quartered" like the brute,
  And made the sport of passion; to begin
A life of vassalage, with such a slave
  Yclept as master, claiming from above
The license that Jehovah never gave
Except the iron hand was woven o'er with love—
It is too much! God's justice is not lame.
  Hypocrisy may steal and wear the cloak,
And don the ermine, with its fair, false claim;
  With crucifix and litany may croak;
But Time o'ertakes it and it falls to earth
  Like Judas on its immolating sword,
  And it must learn to curse its hour of birth.
It is the pledge of destiny—the stern, unwritten word.

THE LANDING OF THE SPANIARDS.

The Courier*, new laden from the coast,
Has hastened to the council of the King
With most portentious tidings : picture-prints

---

* Courier, a courier came daily from the coast, and Couriers from different parts of the Empire; their only script was the picture prints; rude, it is true, and yet wonderful in conveying the different shades of meaning.

That tell of boats that float upon the wing ;
And pale-faced warriors, clad in shining scales.
The monarch hears with trembling ; he has long
Looked for the coming of great Quetzalcoatl,
And, though he felt his nation to be strong,
Yet had he feared his reign would be the last.
The oracles had read him overcast,
With some impending destiny—the ruse
Which priests have always found to compass their abuse.

The chiefs of church and state are all convened
    To canvas, and compare their theories,
And much of wisdom surely can be gleaned
    From these firm-visaged counsellors of his;
And Montezuma* is the first to speak—
    His dark, sad eyes are beautifully bright ;
He was not philosophic like the Greek,
    And yet his words made glitter of the night :

"We swing upon the hinges of our fate,
Most reverend priests and worthy counsellors,
And it is well we counsel and conform
Our future to the fashion of events.
The rising sun has sent inquiring rays
For many years, to greet our coming god,
And lo ! he now turns back from Tlapalan ;

———

*Montezuma's protest against human sacrafice though not literally fact, so far
as the historic record is concerned, is hazarded as not inconsistent with his historic character.

"And what must we, but welcome his advance?
Ye long have held me kindred of the gods ;
Yet I deny me what your partial eyes
Have kenned upon my unassuming face.
I am as other men, though more advanced ;
And if great Quetzalcoalt takes back my crown,
I bow in humble vassalage to him.
For what am I, to question his advance?
A moth, upon the torches' fervent ray;
An anthill, at the foot of 'Catapetl.

And I have sometimes thought most worthy priests,
That we have drawn the lightning from the cloud
By a mistaken worship of the gods.
No one will question my religious zeal,
For I brought many victims to the block ;
But human blood doth have a subtile voice
That reaches ears our eyes have never seen ;
And though the itztli opens to the heart,
Some heart may beat far out in open space
That whispers its avengement on the air.
Our gods have brought us victory, 'tis true ;
And yet, great Nezahualcoyolt did spurn
The shedding of all human blood, to gods ;
And when great Quetzalcoatl was on the earth,
Our gods were satisfied with other blood.
The angels of the mighty past cry out
Against the damning practice .   Why not now,

"For once and all, wash off our bloody hands?
These human cries pierce farther than we know ;
These human souls may ride into the sun ;
We cannot claim his broad, uncumbered breast,
To the exclusion of the rest of earth.
The god of earth and air may come to judge
At this dark moment for this very sin ;
Then let us look him boldly in the face,
And if we have offended, make amends ;
If our mistaken zeal has overdone,
Surely his heart will cover up our faults,
And we may thus propitiate his wrath."

Then rose the ancient High Priest, Tlalocan,*
And in his sternest manner, thus he spake :
"Great Montezuma !   king, of earthly kings !
The heart of Tlalocan is bruised and broke
To hear the words his monarch has vouchsafed
Such sacrilege belongeth not to kings ;
Great Huitzilopotchli must, indeed, be strayed,
Or. he will shake his thunders on the earth,
And, strike the Aztecs from the face of him.
War is the wastage of all human flesh,
And whether man be stricken on the field,
Or, with the sacred itztli, offered up,
The measure must be met with human blood .

'Tlalocan, Prescott has not left on record the name of the High Priest, and
the name given, I have thought in keeping with the Aztic language.

"Thy empire has been purchased at this price,
And cannot otherwise perpetuate.
The earth and heaven, both have set their mark
Upon the bosom of the placid lake ;
And by the coming of those fiery stars,
That flashed their baleful faces in the sky,
All omenous that anger brooded o'er,
The gods have read the purpose of your soul ;
And thus forwarn you that you must retract.
They cry for victims and must be appeased ;
They gave you conquest without stay or stint,
When you did furnish, full to their desire ;
But there are few within the shambles now,
And they must be replenished, or the doom,
That has forshadowed on the Eastern sky,
Will flash and fall upon your naked head.
Great Quetzalcoatl will come and strike you down,
And grind you into ashes in his wrath."

Then spoke the sturdy Counselor Teuhtlile* :
" Tlalocan holds the nearest place to heaven,
And in his zeal, doth sound the ready key
That rhythms with your empire. We must suit
Our action with his words, or we are lost.
These pale-faced warriors must be met with alms ;
The gods must be appeased with fresh supplies.

---

*Teuhtlile, the Embassador sent to meet Cortez. He was high in the coun-
cils of the King.

"Let me, myself, go down upon the coast,
And with our ready painters bring you back
A full account of what we look upon.
And if, perchance, these be the van of him
Whose coming we have watched these many years,
Then will we counsel further the emprise,
And in the watch and wake of all events,
Be not o'ertaken, but forestall the time."

"Your counsel has the sanction it desires;
I would not measure lances with the gods,"
The monarch answered :   "In the dust I bend,
And plead the weakness of a human heart.
The South shall furnish victims for the block ;
And Teuhtlile shall repair him to the coast ;
The dread monition of the flaming stars
May be evaded with our ready zest.
Our gold and precious stones, with lavish hand,
Shall be poured out to coy them from our track;
For what are all the earth's indulgences,
Against the smiling favor of the gods ?"

" Repair thou to the coast, my good Teuhtlile,
With plenteous retinue, and goodly stores ;
With cotton fabrics of the latest cast ;
With shields and cuirasses inlaid with gold ;
The burnished mirror of the fervent sun ;
The silver shining circlet of the moon ;

" With robes of feather-cloth made rich with pearls ;
And other trophies that your tact shall find.
Receive them kindly, as becomes their state ;
And let thy wisdom gather in the full,
Their purpose and intent upon our land ;
It may fall out they are as other men,
Unsanctioned at the chambers of the gods,
Yet must our moderation pave the way,
Till we have fully compassed their intent."

So said, so done ; the embassy went forth
   To meet the wily Spaniard on the coast;
They little dreamed of what a forest fox
   They had to meet ; they little knew the boast
That hung upon the challenge of their fate.
   Their superstitions made them ready prey;
They opened wide their hospitable gate,
   And gave the jewel of their life away.
It mattered little how they forced it back,
   And tried to parley with their destiny ;
The hungry lion was upon their track,
   And they were lost forever and for aye.

Done in the name of Christ ? Oh, spare the word !
   Let not the Nazarene be buffeted ;
Gold was the souvenir ; the pitying Lord
   Was, with this nation, just as deeply bled.
Their superstitions were the ready springs

The Spaniards played upon to break their hearts ;
Deceit, as damnable as serpents' stings,
  Barbed with its cruel spines their poisoned darts.

The embassy returned, and others went;
  Still could they not force back this coming cloud—
The steady purpose and the black intent,
  That wove with cunning fingers at their shroud.
Had Spain come as the Pilgrims at Cape Cod,
  Or Penn upon the Delaware, to lead
The Aztec back to fatherhood and God,
  And let their sturdy manhood for them plead,
How ready could their faces been upturned,
  And hearts been melted into Christian mold !—
The brand of hell was on their bare backs burned,
  And they were ground to ashes for their gold !

Did Christ e'er suffer such supreme disgrace ?
  Or on the cross ; or in Gethsemane ?
Did heavier drops of blood stand on his face
  Than there were forced by this foul treachery?
Oh ! how the patient Nazarene must bend
  And break beneath fresh crosses every day—
Fresh Judases betraying him as friend,
  And scorpions to sting him in the way !
Thank God ! the time is coming when, as Judge,
  The Man of Sorrows, ermined and supreme,
No longer as a packhorse or a drudge,
  Shall hold the scales and watch the balance beam !

How heavy did he make the widow's mite ;
    How do the tears of men bend down the scale ;
How ponderous is a pennyweight of right ;
    How do the little things of life prevail !
The Spanish Conquest, sometime, will be tried
    Against the heart Malinche* threw away,
And Aztec's tears be placed against your pride.
    O Hispagniola ! you will rue the day—
A feather and a mountain to be weighed—
    How shall the beam fly up at your disgrace,
How shall your curse, a hundred fold, be paid,
    And what a glory light up Aztlan's face!

You came, like tender shepherds to the fold,
    Yet, like a wolf, you tore the frighted flock ;
You kissed but to decoy them from their gold ;
    Your seeming calm was but the earthquake's shock.
Your empty babble of the cross and Christ,
    Was but the mask to cover your deceit;
Your hearts were canker, but your words enticed,
    And *never* did a fouler scheme make conquest more
        complete.

Not Aztlan, with her bare and bleeding breast,
    Alone, hath felt thy treachery too late ;
Columbus, in his chains and sorely pressed,
    Bends to thy penalty for being great.

——
Malinche, Interpreter and Mistress of Cortez.

A thousand white-robed saints with bony palms
  Shake their accusing fingers in thy face;
Their bodies burned, their souls changed into psalms,
  To chant in mournful cadence thy disgrace.

ARRIVAL OF THE SPANIARDS AT MEXICO.

November comes as Autumn's requiem,
  To sigh and sough the harvest, and the field,
The winged ecstatics mourn, and then are dumb,
  And life and growth in full submission yield.
Mexitli is not altogether clad
  In nature's winding sheet of yellow leaves ;
And yet her year is getting old and sad,
  And youth and fruitage at his bedside grieves.
As on the lingering footsteps of the year—
  A stranger and the Winter, hand in hand,
Both on the threshold as two ghosts appear.
  One strikes the orbit with its wasting sand,
The other coils around the nation's throat ;
  The nation and the year together die ;
Both on the waste of time are set afloat,
  And sound alike death's mighty mystery.

In all the glitter at his vast command,
  Went Montezuma to receive his guests ;
If gold be great, then was it truly grand.
  The royal plume upon his forehead rests ;

His feet pressed soles of heavy beaten gold ;
　　His cloak and anklets sprinkled o'er with pearls,

And only noble hands are left to hold
The blazing palanquin.　Like titled Earls,
They guard the skirts of royalty from stain
Against the common people ; all the same
As in our ripened age.　'Tis hard to gain
Much on the　sodden march of royalty,
Where accident supplants all other claim.
The monarch in the easy prime of life,
But lightly bronzed.　The glowing, mellow hue
That lit his cheek, seemed borrowed from the sun,
And shadowing a heart that beat as true
To God and country as he knew their names,—
As any monarch that e'er wore a crown.
His open-hearted welcome, like himself,
Was, as the hardy yoeman,　bare and brown.

He felt that he was meeting destiny,
　　Yet, to its solving, he would bend the knee
With dignity and grace ; not turn away,
　　But face it with a ready, cheerful glance,
And meeting night, surcharge it with the day ;
　　And grasping, break, if possible, the lance
That he felt sure was leveled at his breast.
　　He did not know the Inquisition stood,
With rack and torture at his very gate ;

That it had traveled half the world for blood
To whet its throat for St. Bartholomew
  And came with ravening appetite for him.
Those wary messengers he little knew,
Or those brown eyes would suddenly grown dim,
And the warm heart would furnaced up its heat ;
  And he would grappled at its very throat ;
And man to man, and blood to blood, would meet,
  And not a plume above one corselet float
To bear the story back of it to Spain.
  They were not schooled in all the arts of war,
Nor were they wise in all the world's deceit ;
  Yet would they fought beneath their fated star,
And challenged every stubborn step, though it had proven
  vain.

But in this fleecy covering, the wolf
  So hid its teeth that it was at the door
Before they dreamed of treachery. The gulf
  Lay many leagues behind their foes ; its shore
And all the distance had been gained by stealth.
  Tlascala had been humbled on the march,
And promised spoils from Montezuma's wealth ;
  But they had reached the keystone of the arch,
At superstition's beck. The Aztec's gods
Had chained their valor, or their greater odds
  Would crushed the viper, as it should have been,
  And left it to a purer age, to seek a common kin.

The Monarch gave them hostelry and cheer,
   Food of the rarest and the sparkling pulque,
And quarters for their troopers, all quite near
   To his own palace gates. The very bulk
Of his well-laden markets was thrown down
   To their repletion, for their loaded board.
They fared as princes favored of the crown,
   Of all the best the Kingdom could afford.
The fair Malinche was interpreter,
   And Montezuma spoke to them through her.

He told them of the mighty Quetzalcoatl,
And how he recognized them as his kin ;
He thought he had their history, the whole
Vast riddle of their ancient origin.
" I rule a mighty nation," quoth the King.
" All Anahuac is subject to my sway ;
And yet, I recognize that you have come
From the strong palace of a mightier lord,
To whom I bend as subject ; and with you
We now will sway the scepter of his will.
We long have watched his coming from the East,
And now that he has sent his messengers,
Our hearts are ready for his wise commands.
We would have urged your coming on before,
But that we heard of tales of cruelty,
Which, haply we may now believe as false,
We welcome you with all our open hearts,

"And hope you may enjoy our humble fare.
We are not wise, as you are, for our lives
Have not caught wisdom from the fountain head,
And hung upon the lips of Quetzalcoatl;
Yet are we cousins in the faded past,
    And welcome you as brothers and as friends."

How caught the Spanish Chieftain at the words !
    How did he gloat upon this artifice!
How useless hung their heavy-hilted swords
    That they should win a nation at this price !
With what a care he turned the dusty past,
    To cover up the semblance of disguise;
And fix their superstition still more fast,
    That he might clutch and carry home the prize.

" There *is* grandeur in the tented field ;
    The bivouac and the smoldering camp-fires."
The human soul unconsciously must yield
    To its supremest charm, where man aspires
To meet his fellow-man at one great bar ;
    And " valor speaks to valor " of its claim,
In all the panoply of stubborn war,
    And drops the gauntlet in a nation's name.
It may be terrible, but it is grand
    To see the banners flaunting in the breeze ;
To hear the bugle blare and stern command;
    And see opposing forces strive to seize

From Nature's stern arbitrament of force
  The laurel that shall deck the victor's brow;
And turn the stream of nations from its course.
  The cutting of new sod by such a plow
May tear up all the tender ties of life ;
  And hearts be turned to ashes in its path ;
These are the ponderous incidents of strife,
  And made legitimate when wrath meets wrath ;
But when the assassin creeps into our hearts,
  And draws around him all their sanctities,
And he becomes a parcel of our parts,
  And all we have or claim are made as his,
What human brush can paint the upraised hand
  That smites our confidence at such an hour?
What simile can human tongue command ?
  It is, indeed, beyond our mortal power.
We talk of devil, but the word is tame ;
  It cannot reach the climax we have sought ;
It only frets us into hotter flame,
  And beggars all the litany of thought.

I do not claim that Cortez was not brave ;
  Nor would I tear one laurel from his brow.
I only claim he stole the devil's glaive ;
  He held it then, and let him hold it now.
The issues of their lives are both with God,
  The brown-eyed Monarch and the dark-eyed Knight.
The flowers of charity should strew the sod

Above them both ; yet, Cosmos ! was it right ?
O world of human hearts and human lives !
Was Montezuma worthy of this fate?
O world of husbands ! world of tender wives !
Behold your Aztlan ! bleeding, desolate,
And say, if all their multiple of sins,
Though they be blacker than the blackest night,
Were worthy of the end that now begins
To grind them down to powder? Was it right
For Spain to steal the scepter from the hand
That held it out in welcome to their doors,
And poured their treasures out as free as sand,
And oped with lavish all their loaded stores ;
To steal the key of superstition's gate,
And break the lock upon their hard-earned gold,
And, fattening at their table, steal their plate,
And feasting on their lambs to steal their fold ;
To make a prison of the room he gave
In which to hold the Monarch as a slave?
O pitying God ! thy thunderbolts were scarce.
Why crushed they not this hell-begotten farce?

And when the Aztecs, goaded to the quick
By the proud insolence of such a horde,
Could bear no longer parley, but were sick
Of such a visitor at such a board,
And rose en masse to crush the viper's fang,
They bring the Monarch out to face the crowd,

And plead for their immunity ; the pang
  That wrung his breast (for he, indeed, was proud)
Was like an arrow in his royal heart ;
  And yet he prayed for their forgiveness then,
And like a martyr bravely bore their part —
  Search history ; and find out greater men,
And they are less forgiving. There he stood,
  His nation thronged before him, in its wrath ;
Yet did he plead, before this multitude,
  To spare the serpent, now across their path ;
He could not name a promise not unbroke,
  He could not offer one excuse for time,
He could not tell them why to hold their stroke,
  He plead for hands scarred over with their crime.

Did ever charity reach loftier height ?
  Can Christian Spain outshine this sad, brown face?
How many souls in Christiandom, as white,
  Would faced his countrymen, from such a place?
Great Montezuma ! where shall we find room !
  When Spain has such a multitude of saints
To save your enemies, you courted doom,
  Yet would not kiss the cross with your complaints ;
Therefore, anathema!—It will not do,
  To pass a heretic at Heaven's gate ;
You held no mumbled crusifix to view—
  The Infallible has said it, you must wait.
Wait for a riper age to touch the chord

That quivers, all unconsciously, your praise ;
When justice, *only*, draws the tardy sword,
And Earth's abhorrence covers those old days
With its repentent ashes, then my King
May rest his memory upon stubborn facts
Nor minstrels falter when they fain would sing
Their elegies implanted with *his* acts.
The Holy Inquisition, from old Spain,
And St. Bartholomew, from "Ma belle France,"
The hissing fagots of sweet Mary's reign—
These million martyrs, with their melting glance,
Look at *his* agony, across the sea,
Who, blind in superstition, groped his way
O'er harmless victims and much misery
To where the rays were slanting into day.
In Europe's face the star of Bethleham,
With its benignant splendor, shed its light ;
These but the groping nomads of old Shem,
Lost in the meshes, of a rayless night.
Those, neath the palm of Earth's philosophy ;
These on the torchless desert, not a star
To guide them through life's potent mystery ;
Those bringing all the wisdom from afar,
Though Montezuma's sins had cried to Heaven
In a far greater stress; yet what were they,
Paling his cruelties, and still forgiven,
To pour out greater vials the next day ?
O Spain ! you lent the sanction of your name,

To cover up the foulest deed of time;
Upon your skirt is fastened this great shame,
And nation never wore the brand of a more causeless
    crime.

DEATH OF MONTEZUMA.

One sad, sad task, awaits my faltering pen,
And I have done.   One flower upon *his* grave,
Who in his dying could, alas ! not save
His country from the vulturous maw of men.
They played upon the monarch with their arts,
    Till he became a captive in their hands;
It was consistent with their *Christian* hearts
    That their good host should follow their commands.
They said their *Christian* lord across the sea
    Must have his treasure for their *Christian* use.
All this was bitter, yet, he did agree,
    And bent a patient knee to their abuse.

They struck their temples, and the red, right hand
    Of Aztlan rose upon them.   They could bear
To see their monarch littled, and their land
    Made tribute to a stranger ; but, beware
Stern warriors of Castile ! touch not their gods.
    The hearts of Aztlan are but human hearts,
And at some shrine the whole creation nods;
    Invade the sanctum, and the whole man starts.

Las Casas* would have won them with his love—
　The potent key that opens every gate.
Let not deceit claim sanction from above;
　It may assist upon the wheels of fate,
But what Spain offered through such legatees
　Was worse than powder on the bated flame.
To gather fruit from such ill-freighted trees,
Was worse than stealing nightmare from a dream.

In Christ's good name they stole the monarch's gold ;
　They changed the name of Christ to treachery ;
They gathered all the spoils their hands could hold,
　And pointed to their Master on the tree.
Their Master?　No ! since Lucifer was hurled
　Down from the shining chambers of the just
To vent his spleen upon a new-made world,
　He never had a worthier task in trust,
Than that he gave to Spain's inglorious knights,
To rob this people of their vested rights.

The people gather at the palace gates,
　And vengeance writes itself upon each face ;
Their generosity no longer waits,
　They spit upon, and spurn the outraged place.
It harbors those who wrote themselves as knaves
　Upon the pliant tablets of their lives,

* Las Casas, a worthy Spanish Padre, who was constantly protesting against the villanous conduct of the cavaliers. Prescott pays him a glowing tribute.

And now the incensed nation only craves
　　Deliverance for their children and their wives.
They know the belching cannon of the knights
　　Will make sad havoc in their stately host ;
They know that Spain and Fate to-day unite ;
　　They know, if fortune fails them, all is lost ;
But they can bear no longer to be torn,
And swear by all the gods to pluck this thorn.
The Spaniards see their perfidy, too late ;
And call great Montezuma to the gate.
" Why are my people here to-day in arms ?
These stranger friends are still my welcome guests ;
They soon will turn them backward to their homes.
Shall we raise hands against great Quetzalcoatl ?
We fight against the gods ?　Lay down your arms !
Go to your homes, and all shall yet be well,
And peace shall reign in all Tenochtitlan * ! "
They bent before him reverently at first.
It was a moment—then their anger burst :
" Base Aztec ! woman ! coward ! sneaking slave !
The whites have made a puppet of your name !
Talk not of fighting 'gainst our honored gods ;
We soil their sacred robes if we submit ! "
A cloud of stones and arrows flew the air ;
And Montezuma fell a victim of *their* rage and *his* de-
　　spair.

---

*Te-noch-ti-tlan, the Aztec for the city of Mexico.

His heart had broke when he beheld the throng,
For he was burning with his country's wrong;
And when the missiles smote his fevered crest,
His very soul was reaching out for rest.
They only helped to roll the burden off,
    So long imprinted on his saddened face—
It was *too* much to hear his people scoff—
    He fell ; and they removed him from the place.
He never rose again, nor wished to rise ;
    He made no effort to outlive his land ;
He felt *his* weakness, and he heard *her* cries ;
    He saw *her* sinking with *his* wasting sand.
He knew his enemies had stole the garb
    Of gods to fasten on him their deceit ;
That they had stung the nation with their barb,
    And he would not survive its sore defeat.
He felt their scoffings were deserved of him,
    For he should gathered wisdom with his years ;
He saw his weakness when his sight was dim,
    And poured his wasting moments out in tears.

They called the Priest to shrive him for his death—
    The worthy Monk Olmedo* takes his palms ;
It is in vain ; his very latest breath
    Repulses all their uninvited alms.
He dies an Aztec—honor to his name !—

---

*Olmedo, a priest of that easy piety that characterized the cavalier, ready to grant absolution in case of all excesses.

And spurns the symbols that have crushed him down.
What mockery when he is all aflame
  With their abuses ! Give him back his crown,
His country's honor, and its hard-earned gold.
  But force no wormwood to his fevered lips ;
His hand is pulseless, and will soon be cold ;
  His life was shadow ; and his death —eclipse.

Great are the consolations of the cross—
  The Father-Son of Calvary, and time.
Their glory compensates a kingdom's loss ;
  But piety must not be wed to crime.
Did all the roses blossom from the cross,
  And all the thorns grow out upon the waste?
Then were the metal guarded from the dross,
  And every crust be suited to our taste ;
But bitter-sweet is all the book of life,
  And thorns and roses crowd the tangled way ;
And good and evil, always, are at strife—
  Night always dogs the footsteps of the day.
Yet "figs cannot be gathered from the thorn,"
  Nor "grapes from thistles," says the patient Lord—
One great, good life, like a new angel born,
  Is the most potent sermon ever heard.

The hands that smote the Monarch in the face
  Did honor to his ashes, cold and dead.
Their anger was rubbed out, and not a trace

Was left, as with their slow and measured tread
They bore his sacred ashes to the tomb
  Within the walls of old Chapultepec,
Where stately trees, and flowers perennial bloom,
  And, all the pulses of their lives in check,
Bow down to kiss the shrine of memory.
  The sacred hush of death comes none too oft
To still the fevered brain and make us free—
  It is a gentle hand, and moves so soft
That it compensates all our misery
  By chaining all the lions of our life
And placing durance on the throbbing drum
  That marshals us to earth's unpitying strife.
  How should we reverence the hand that strikes our pas-
    sions dumb !

Cortez and Montezuma; Aztlan, Spain—
  The very mingling of these words is pain.
The one, bold, cold, unscrupulous and brave,
  And making of each obstacle a slave ;
Seeking *his* glory in the name of Christ,
  To gain his ends unfaithful to each tryst.—
The fault is with the ethics of his race,
  Which justify the means for *any* end,
And leave the moral aspect without place,
  And to the foulest acts their ready sanction lend.
The thought of holding man to his account,
  And throwing merit against circumstance,

Of cleansing souls at one great common fount,
    Of holding out to man an equal chance —
These things were not considered in the least.
    The glory of himself and Spain were first ;
All the excesses pardoned by the Priest
    Weaned the poor soul from any moral thirst.
A golden apple trembled on the limb,
    And he must pluck it, at whatever cost.
What matter whose?--it should belong to him ;
    It was too tempting, and must not be lost :
The wall that lay before it must be scaled,
    The owner of the field must be destroyed,
And if his *prowess*, in the effort failed,
    Deceit and *treachery* must be employed.
The unbridled passions of the human soul
    Linked with the crucifix in his emprise.
The lion, loosened and in full control—
    The semblance of the Lamb to Aztlan's eyes :
A faithful offspring of the Papish loins,
    The features of the Church in duplicate,
Though baser metals pass for golden coins,
    Only earth's charity can make brave Cortez great.

But Montezuma conquers all our thought—
    Tenochtitlan and old Chapultepec.
No greener shrine for memory can be sought ;
    The heart and conscience both alike bedeck
The unfading spectre of a soul sincere,

Who tugged at destiny against the dark—
The hand, unconscious, drops its laurels here.
  His brown hands could not helm the fateful bark
Against the baleful breakers of old Spain ;
  Yet, who *is* proof against the foils of men.
His life is but a psalmody of pain.
  What soul unmoved can touch it with the pen ?
The link that bound the old world with the new,
  With pure and patient hands, might been upturned,
And every missing chapter brought to veiw
  By Clio gathered, and again inurned
In history's cloister ; Egypt and Aztlan
  Strike palms upon the bridges of the years ;
But Spain denies the privilege to man,
  And fills the vacuum with a nation's tears.
O Monarch of the fading, mighty past !
  Great Montezuma ! we are wed to thee.
Back of thy name the ocean is so vast
  That we can only write—Eternity,
And leave the secret in thy broken breast.
  We would that we could taken thy warm palm,
Held out in welcome from the mellow West,
  And poured upon thy stricken life the balm
Of real enlightenment ; and point thee back,
  Over the ridges of the years, to God ;
To where your people lost the beaten track,
  And ever afterward were left to plod.
Those great sad eyes, once filled with light from Heaven,

Would shone like diamonds when they found the way,
And every fibre of thy nature striven
    To turn thy nation's darkness into day.
Alas! 'tis vain! we beat the empty air.
Our tears are mingled with thy wasting breath;
We *all* are torn with thy warm heart's despair,
    And mourn with Aztlan at thy fateful death.

CONCLUSION.

From sire to son the stern bequeathment falls
    Of some misguided action in the past,
And, though our nature with the victim calls
    And we are smitten with his overcast,
Still are we weak against the wheels of fate,
Which leaves the pensioner thus desolate.

The by-ways of the father must turn back
    Sometime upon the highway that he left;
Though dark and sinuous may be the track,
    And life of all its luster be bereft,
Still hangs the heavy impulse on the soul,
Unsatisfied, till it shall reach its goal.

The destiny was hard that brought proud Spain
    Upon the fading summerland of gold;
Its retribution is no less a pain;
    The grip of fate, so pulseless and so cold,
Brings back the shudder to the human heart;

Humanity is wounded with *each* part
That feels the puncture of her cruel blade.
Nor is the censure less upon the hand
That strikes *so* hard to force the debt thus paid.
The tender conquest of some heathen land
The brightest jewel is, of any crown—'
God never licensed human hand to strike a foe when
    down.

When Spain's recruited army turned them back
    To glut their ire on Guatamozin's head,
There never was a deeper furrowed track,
    More thickly cindered with the myriad dead ;
And when at last his bloody sceptre fell,
Tenochtitlan was likest to a hell.

The brave barbarian was put to rack
    To force divulgence of his scattered gold.—
Is there a garment of a deeper black,
    To cover up the fingers that could hold
Such hellish orgies after all the past ?
The palm is thine, O Spain ! and hold it to the last !

Yet one more turn upon the screw of time :
    Thy red, right hand must slay this waif of fate ;
And thou must put the climax to the crime,
    And crush the heart thou has made desolate.
Enough ! thou art the acme of the earth—
May God's great pity ever spare thy duplicated birth !

No, no, not Spain ! *her* better angel waits,
    And *has* been waiting all these weary years
For Castellar to open wide her gates,
    That she may wash her garments with her tears ;
But priestcraft, Rome, or demon, all the same—
    That makes a desert of her rich champaign ;
And sends her forth through history, so tame.
It is, her evil genius ; but it is not Spain.

———

As Kohen prophesied, their race was run—
    Their error cleaved upon them as a curse ;
The fading phalanx of the Summer sun
    Has crossed the borders of the universe.
We only catch the shadow of their flight ;
They pass out with the sunset into night.

MALINCHE.

INTRODUCTION.

I may properly place " Malinche " as supplementary to
" Montezuma," as dealing with characters coincident to,
and cotemporaneous with those concerned in the " Conquest," and also as covering a period subsequent to, and
immediately succeeding the Conquest.

To the student of history, Malinche (in her position of
interpreter during the entire period of the Conquest) presents at once so much that is unique and charming, and
yet such a sad commentary on the criminal practices of
the sixteenth as well as the nineteenth centuries, that I
have often wondered that a stronger and more practiced
hand has not ere this claimed the privilege of champion-
ship.

According to Prescott, she was born in the town
of Painnalla, Province of Coatzacualco, in the southeast-
ern extremity of what is now Mexico; that she was the
daughter of a Cacique (a sort of provincial Governor)
and prospective heiress to large estates; that after the
death of her father, her mother, with indecent haste,
forms another union, and in time presents the stepfather
with a son; that they jointly combine to be rid of Ma-

linche, whom they sell to itinerant traders; and, to cover their device, they pretend that she is sick and use the child of a servant for their criminal pantomime; the child dies, thus completing the deception, except the hypocritical mourning to which this unnatural mother is said to have been equal.

Malinche is sold by the traders to the Cacique of Tabasco, and reaches maturity about the time of the Conquest. She seems to have been a favorite in the house of the Cacique, which would indicate that he had become acquainted with her origin, and after the surrender of the town to Cortez, she is one of the twenty female slaves presented to the Conqueror and his allies.

Either from enlarged opportunities or her natural aptness, and probably both, she is found by Cortez to be just the person he needs for interpreter. Mutual attraction leads them into the closest relations, and it is but just to Malinche to state that there is no indication of her knowledge of the Conqueror's wife in Cuba, until she arrives at the Capitol. There is also nothing to indicate more than a momentary estrangement between Malinche and Catalina.

Catalina lived but about three months after her arrival at Mexico; and it seems that Malinche assumes the same relations as before, when Cortez journeys South, where in time they reach the precincts of the maiden's nativity, and she meets her mother, after all the years of their cruel separation. Here the beautiful sincerity of the Christianity she had espoused, shines forth as she quiets her mother's fears, and professes to doubt her mother's original intent to sell her. She loads her mother with jewels and seems to cherish no feeling not consistent with the warmest relations of daughter and mother.

The statement soon after is, that Cortez presents her to Don Xamarillo with all the sanction of marriage, and he enriches her with some of the largest estates in her native province; and there the historic account closes. Incidentally, it is mentioned that a son was born during the period of this *affaire du coeur.*

I stated that the historic account closes here, but M. Charny and others enlarge on the traditionary feeling of South Eastern Mexico, and if we may credit his statements (and many times tradition carries more heart and more of the essential elements of truth in it than the cold pencil of history), Malinche is so woven into the social structure as to become almost the patron saint of that part of the country.

And Prescott (rather inclined to the fruit than the blossom of history) speaks of Malinche as being reverently held by the Aztec descendants as the guardian angel of Chapultepec.

I have endeavored thus to present the salient features of this part of the historic drama, adding and enlarging only as it became necessary to connect the events and do justice to the fair subject of the endeavor ; and whatever criticism may be offered, I can, without hesitancy, claim the credit of candor and a desire to eliminate from all the facts of the case the plain, unvarnished truth.

I began at first to write the idyl in nine-syllabic measure, but soon found myself cramped in expression, and in recopying I have thrown off restraint and used the double terminal with both nine and ten syllables, having no desire and finding no occasion to use the eight syllable measure which Longfellow has so immortalized in the " Song of Hiawatha."

The sacred relations of man and wife, like those of any other *sacrament* entered into voluntarily, are no less binding in the *spirit* than in the *letter* of the law ; and it is a gratifying truth that the statutes of many of the States of the Union are being so remodeled as to recognize the *fact*, rather than the *form* of marriage ; and the tendency is certainly toward the correction of many abuses, as leading to a more enlarged knowledge of social responsibilities.

As long as the sad story of Malinche has a present application, and may be said to be the perspective of the grossly distorted foreground of our social structure, so long will its rehearsal have its use in the world ; and I only regret that a stronger hand and a more perfect pen might not have been loaned to its portrayal.

H. H. RICHMOND.

MALINCHE.

Old Painnalla of Coat-za-cual-co,
Passing down the road of the "Conquest,"
Through the silent portals of Lethe,
Was greatest of Mexican hamlets ;
The birthplace of brown-eyed Malinche,
Whom the Spaniards call Dona Marina ;
And the noble Cacique, great Tezpitla,
With his shrew of a wife, Zunaga—
All are names deserving of story,
For they cling to the garment of greatness.

A daughter is born to Zunaga,
And the worthy Cacique Tezpitla,
Though he warms to the little stranger,
Had hoped that the gods would have given
A son and Cacique for the province.
They named their young daughter Malinche ;
The priest called the gods to protect her,
And sprinkled her brow and her bosom
With water, the purest of emblems ;
Commends her to Tez-cat-li-po-ca,

The soul of the earth and the heavens ;
To Quet-zal-coatl, god of the harvest ;
And at all the shrines with their homage,
They offered the richest of jewels.

Tezpitla soon sleeps with his fathers,
And Malinche, too young to have known him,
Has hardly begun with her prattle,
Ere he passes away to the sunset,
To the palace of gold Tonatu',
Where his warriors had gone on before him
To their rest, in the dazzling chambers
That shine from the face of the day god.

Zunaga a little while murmurs,
And mourns at the chieftain's departure,
When Mohotzin, a friend of Tezpitla
(Who had shared oft times in his battles
And sat many times at his table),
In sympathy visits the widow ;
And his sympathy turns to wooing,
His wooing and winning are easy.
For Zunaga (the name of the faithless)
Yields a ready ear to his sighing,
And pity is parent of loving.
The bride takes the place of the widow,
And the funeral leads to the wedding.

A son is soon born to Mohotzin,
And the sire with the faithless Zunaga,
Bend their heads to the hurt of the helpless,
To disherit the artless daughter;
She sends up inquisitive glances,
To the guilty eyes of her parents.
Thus the perfect faith of our childhood,
Stands to smite at the evil endeavor,
Yet how is it cruelly wounded
By the cunning hand of its kindred!

She is sold as a slave to the merchants,
Whose itinerant traffic encounters
This cruel and conscienceless couple.
Scarcely five years the miniature maiden,
When decoyed from her favorite pastimes,
Under guise of a frolicsome journey;
She is hurried away into bondage,
To gain the estate for her brother.
And all this is done under shadow
To cover the basest of actions.
Malinche is said to be dying,
The mother is bent at the bedside,
Where is laid the child of a servant;
It dies, to complete the deception,
And Zunaga bewails, as is fitting
In well painted actions, the daughter.
The funeral pageant is greater

Than the one attending Tezpitla ;
And thus, did the misnomered mother
Strive to hide the print of her sinning.

How fares it with bonnie Malinche,
Thus stung in the morn of her childhood ?
The merchants have gone to Tabasco,
The slaves are the bearers of burden,
The maid is thus borne from her kindred.
She, too young to plead for ransom,
Little heeds the force of her venture ;
And in time, they have traversed the river,
And have reached the town of Tabasco.
The merchants immured in their traffic,
Sell the maid to a wealthy landlord,
The worthy Cacique of the province.

Thus cruelly shorn of her birthright,
Malinche grows up as a servant
In the house of this wealthy master,
The playmate and charm of his children.
She gathers the boon of contentment
With the easy faith of her childhood.
Her mother is almost forgotten,
When a former nurse of Zunaga,
Having served the time of her ransom,
Has sought the Cacique for employment.
She knows the whole piteous story,

Of the maid and her heartless mother ;
Her soul is drawn back to the maiden,
And she knows, with the whole of her nature,
That this is her old master's daughter.
And Malinche, across the threshold,
Calls back all the thoughts of her childhood,
And each feels the grasp of the other,
And the past is all plain to Malinche.

The noble Cacique of Tabasco
Heard all of the pitiful story,
And swore, by the gods, to avenge her
" Of her cruel and faithless mother,
With her heart as hard as the itztli,
The sanctified blade of the prophet."
He would seek the king, Moctheuzoma,
That ruled in the city of temples,
Tenochtitlan, greatest of cities,
And tell him the tale of Malinche,
That all of her wrongs might be righted
And the maiden restored to her birthright.

But, in the white heat of his anger,
A stranger appears at the river—
'Tis the pale-faced chief, and his army,
With his soldiers clad like the fishes,
With the shining scales for their frontlets,
With their weapons charged with the lightning,

Like the thunderbolts of great Thaloc,
With their four-legged gods, like the bison,
With the head of a man in the center,
And the flaming nostril distended,
Breathing fire, like the front of a dragon,
When they shake the earth with their tramping.
Surely these were the legates of heaven,
Great Quetzalcoatl, surely fought with them.
And in vain was the chieftain's endeavor,
Tabasco soon fell to their prowess,
And they must now purchase appeasment.
And the worthy Cacique of Tabasco
Forgets all his pledges of ransom,
And Malinche is one of the twenty,
Of the maids that he gives to Cortez.
As pure as the bright water lily
That shines from the rim of Tezcuco ;
As bright as the rays of Tonatu',
Rising out of the gulf of Mexitli;
As chaste as the moon in its glances,
At the mirroring face of Chalco;
As fresh as the breezes that banquet
The morn in the isles of the spices—
Even such was the Maid of Painnalla,
The beautiful brown-eyed Malinche.

Cortez has been seeking a sponsor
To ravel the intricate language,

When he is informed of the maiden,
And she is first brought to his presence.
A favorite child of the household,
She is robed in the neatest of vestures.
The feather-cloth covers her shoulders,
Her waist is enclosed with a girdle
Holding skirt of the finest of cotton,
Her feet on the daintiest sandals,
Her face, veiled with gossamer pita,
Lends the highest charm to her blushes.

With Aguilar first she converses
‚(He had lived some years with the natives,
Borne ashore where his vessel had stranded).
She had learned all the various shadings,
The many and quaint dialections,
Of the several Anahuac nations ;
And not long till the noble Castilian
Yields its palm to her ready conquest.
The mighty commander, brave Cortez,
With his piercing dark eyes, was her teacher ;
For love is the aptest of pupils,
And the heart is your ready translator.
The words of the Chief were no longer
The meaningless voice of the stranger,
But the language of Spain and of heaven.

Cortez, cast a thought to the island ;
To his early love, Catalina ;
To the prison of fierce Velasquez ;
His reluctant marriage in Cuba.
Yet, how faithful had been the Dona !
And never yet had been broken
His pledges of perfect devotion ;
But the morals of Hispagniola
Are subject to easiest bending.
The priest giving ready indulgence
To sins that are nearest to nature,
And Malinche, robbed of her birthright
And denied the boon of a mother,
Had only her love to direct her,
Which led her unerring to Cortez ;
He opened his arms to receive her,
(She, the purest jewel of Aztlan)
And, as moth falls into the torchlight,
She fell to his brilliant alluring.

If purest of wifely devotion,
With its love that is *all* of woman,
If the absence of wrong intention
In the innocent glow of nature,
Uninspired by the shadow of evil,
Made her wife, she was wife of Cortez.
Not a whisper of Catalina,
His beautiful wife on the island,

Had the chieftain given the maiden ;
And she felt as free as the water
On the rugged brink of 'Morenci;
As the bee to gather the honey
From the nectaries on the mountains
And the multiple bloom of the valleys.
She thought there was naught to prevent her
From her lavish of love on the Chieftain.

O the faith that is always faultless,
That ever grows up toward Heaven,
(To the center of love returning)
Whence it sprang as seed from the Godhead !
How its track is hounded by evil !
How its purity pants in the darkness !
How it flutters into the pitfalls !
And how its white wings are broken
And its plumage stained and bedraggled!
But 'tis only the earth that despoils it,
To teach it more earnest endeavor,
To lift the wing higher in ether,
And fix the eye firmer on Heaven.

But alas ! for bonnie Malinche ;
Her faith had no heavenly fragrance,
Except in its helpless dependence.
It knew not the way of the angels,
But groped like the vine in the cavern,

Always reaching out for the sunlight,
Always tender and white of fiber.
And the worthy father, Olmedo,
Taught the maid the lore of the ages ;
Taught of life, and death, and the Savior,
And the beautiful boon, resurrection,
And the story of Magdalene,
Of much loving, and much forgiving ;
Yet he whispered naught of the Chieftain,
And the maiden lived on in blindness,
Though " Credos " and " Ave Marias "
Fell as pearls from the lips thus laden
With the story of Jesu' and Mary.
And as Christ touched the lips of childhood
And made them the text of his sermon,
(The innocent sponsors of Heaven)
Malinche, enrapt at the story,
Shined out through her every action,
Translating the life of the God-Son,
To speak in behalf of her people.
She plead for the chiefs of Tlascala—
Las Casas had no abler ally
When he struck the stone heart of Cortez—
And the stonier heart of Castile,
In his earnest prayer for the Aztecs
And the ill-starred King Moctheuzoma.
Her blood gave its ardent petition
In behalf of her race and her people,

Her bronzed hand pressing the balance
On the side of mercy and manhood.

When the light first shines in the cavern
Damp and dark with moldering ages,
It gathers each gleam of the crystals
That cycles have hoarded in brilliance ;
So the heart, groping back to the sunlight,
Over graves of its superstitions,
Throws its shoots through every crevice
That promises health to its fibers.
Thus the virgin soul of Malinche
(The image of God on its tablet)
Made the glow of her first impressions
The heart and the soul of the gospel.

But how cunningly clasp the fetters
That fate has unconsciously molded ;
And yet, how they pinion our passport
On the trend of further indulgence—
The conquest was hardly completed,
And the maid in the fullest enjoyment
Of the treasure she aided to purchase
When the island divulges its secret,
And the wife of his early loving,
And the wife of his after loathing,
Appears at the door of the Chieftain,

O Malinche ! brown-eyed Malinche !
The finger of fate is upon you ;
The wrongs of your conscienceless mother
Were the scar and bane of your *childhood*.
The years with their velveted footfalls
Have forced them far back in the shadows,—
But here comes a heart that is bleeding
For the touch of its earliest treasure.
With an even right you have won it ;
Upon your warm bosom have worn it.
But another, unknown, has possessed it,
And puts forth her hand to recover.
Will you strike at her just petition ?
Love is love ; but hers is the older,
And it has grown sharp with its longing ;
The hunger of years is upon it,
And pleads all the patience of loving.

They met, the brown maid of Painnalla
And the pale, blushing rose of the island,—
Malinche and sad Catalina.
The Dona gave voice to her murmur
In words that were pungent and bitter,
Reproaching the maid for the beauty
That had stolen the heart of her husband.
But Malinche returned no reproaches
When she heard the whole truth from the Dona ;
But her tears, as the dew of the morning,

Which like diamonds filled her dark lashes,
Smote the tender heart of the maiden :

"O maiden, most hard and unconscious !"
Cried Malinche, out of her sobbing,
"Hear the bitter tale of my lifetime ;
And the Heavenly melting of pity
Will fill all the place of your loathing."
Then she told her the whole sad story—
How her cruel mother betrayed her,
How she fell a slave to the Chieftain,
And was called upon to interpret.
"But the heart is easily broken,
Fair maiden ! " Malinche continued.
"And before I knew, I had fallen ;
And I hung on his matchless features,
The wonderful glow of his prowess,
And the liquid flow of his language,
Till I could no longer resist him.
I thought I was free to embrace him,
And I gave my whole life to his keeping.
How I thrilled to his first caressing,
And panted to gather his kisses !
How I hung on the lips of the morning
That shadowed his life with new danger !
Could I die for the love I bore him,
I would pity the weight of the casket
That gave such a featherlike measure ;

Could I stand in the breach of danger
To shelter his form from the missile,
I could mourn that the Father had given
But only one heart for the arrow.
I loved him ! I loved him ! I loved him !
And this is my furtherest pleading."

And long ere Malinche had finished
The Dona had mingled her weeping,
And each held the hand of the other
In truce of their worthless repining ;
And Malinche, as Magdalene,
Would have washed the feet of her Master,
But the Dona rather preferred her
As compainon and friend in pastime ;
So they passed their time in the solace
Of a friendship closely cemented.

But the beautiful flower of the island
Fell a prey to the varying climate
And the dormant love of the Chieftain.
She pointed her white hands to heaven,
And she gave back to Mary Mother
Her tired soul as white as the snowdrift.
The busy brown hands of Malinche
Had never once tired of their office
In smoothing her feverish pillows.
Her fresh, perfect faith pointing upward,

Helped to pinion the soul for its passage.
" Farewell to thee, fair Catalina !
Though you tore my heart with your coming,
You have torn it worse with your going.
May the angels, shrouding your sorrow,
Pour their multiple bliss in your welcome,
And paradise pant with your beauty,
And Heaven, as white as your goodness,
Shine out through the doors for Malinche ;
For I envy your early passage,
And would gladly have gone before you.
I have found earth's love but a fetter
To cripple the wing of our exit."

And after he humbled the Aztecs,
The Chieftain soon turned to the southward,
Still holding the hand of Malinche,
As if the cold palm of the Dona
Had never intruded its presence ;
His memory, cold as her pulses,
Gave hardly a throb at departure,
But Malinche wept o'er her ashes,
And prayed that the blessing of Heaven
Might comfort the soul of the Dona ;
Yet she held not her hand from the Chieftain,
Though she chid with the love of the turtle ;
Yet her heart could not harrow its fallow
Though a hundred-fold lay in the effort.

The ill-fated Chief Guatamozin
(Who succeeded the great Moctheuzoma,
And so stubbornly fought for his people)
Had fared the same fate of the Monarch,
Except that he gazed on the ashes,
And saw the cold ghost of his nation
Pass out through the gates of the sunset,
And all just a little before him.
He attended Cortez on his journey,
With other great men of his people ;
Never man was more loyal to master
Than the throneless King to his Chieftain—
To the cavalcade came a rumor,
That the life of Cortez was endangered
By a plot of the Aztec attendants
(Cortez was the stoniest master,
To the Knights as well as the natives,
And no wonder his life should be threatened.

The scar of a crime on our nature,
With remembrance of wrong we inflicted,
Puts a double watch on our victim ;
We are prone to measure in manner,
Each soul in the pitiful bushel
That holds the shrunk grains of *our* manhood.)
And Cortez turned his eyes for an answer,
To the plot that was laid for his footsteps,
On the staunch Aztec King, Guatamozin ;
He had fought a brave battle for Aztlan,

And the Spaniards had felt his prowess
In the hardly wrenched sword of their triumph;
But when the despair of his nation
Settled down on his heart as a mountain,
No treachery lingered to poison
The flow of his deeply drawn sadness.

Yet, the wrongs he had laid on the people,
Stalked out as a ghost on the Chieftain.
And the sad eyes of poor Guatamozin,
Were his guilty conscience' accuser;
And though not a stain was upon him,
Yet the Chief was condemned by Cortez.
Then Malinche's warm heart overflowing,
When she saw how unjust was the sentence,
Gave its plea with the beautiful pathos
Of the life that is simple and loving.
Though she was baptized as a Christian,
And was charmed with the life of the God-Son,
Yet the water the priest sprinkled on her
Purged not from her veins the warm Aztec
Which, charged with a just indignation,
Poured out on her Chieftain its measure:

" As a faithful God is my witness —
Not a throb of my heart has wasted
Its pulse on the suit of another,
Since you glittered my life with its purchase,

I have loved you too well for my worship,
Which has hardly a God, but my Chieftain;
But I plead for my country and people—
You showed me a Christ that was loving,
Whose life was a psalm of forgiveness,
Who touched the hot lips of our anger
With the tender finger of patience.
I was won by his great example,
It warned the cold stone of the Aztec
With the radient beams of the morning;
It loosened the chains from the ankles
That were swift on errands of mercy;
It tore off the scales from the eyelids
That were blinded with superstition;
Gave freedom to innocent victims,
From the fearful death of the itztli;
And winged back the soul to its manor,
From the desert and dust of the ages.

" But where is the Christ you were pleading—
The merciful God of your banner?
The nails of the cross are your sword points,
And his pleadings the parent of carnage.
His merciful words are but margods,
To hurl on your host to the slaughter.
As I pleaded for Moctheuzoma
That you spare him the shame of his prison,
So I plead for the brave Guatamozin,

Though he fought so hard for the Aztecs,
I would balance my life on his honor.
The traitor is not of such metal,
At your front—in your face—he may strike you ;
But he takes not the night for his helmlet,
Nor is treachery ever his weapon.
Then spare him, my noble Hernando !"
But her prayers were in vain for the victim,
The heart of Cortez was relentless ;
And another brave soul winged its passage,
To try if the gates of the city
Still turn for the broken in spirit.

In time they drew near to Painnalla,
And the tale of her childhood confronts her,
Though she hardly can call up one feature
To gaze on the face of another,
And each say to each, "We are brothers ";
Yet the story has lived with her living,
And been fanned by the fervor of gossip;
And Malinche's warm heart has been shaken,
O'er the bitterest brink of a trial.

Her Chieftain, grown great with his conquest,
Thrusts the knife of his pride to her heartstrings,
In search of some noble alliance ;
And she must be weaned from his wooing.
As only *one* God lighteth Heaven,

She has held the *one* place in his household,
Than which has the earth none more sacred.
Yet the shade of the poor Catalina
Has shown her how weak is the Chieftain,
And the bolt is thus broken in falling ;
Still her whole heart presses the balance,
And a sacred thing was her loving,
For love is the latch-key to Heaven.

But she tries to force back her sorrow
At the sacred shrine of her birthplace ;
And the angels are gentle that hover
At the rustic shade of the hearthstone.
All the sorrow comes out of the shadow,
All the bitterness bathes in the sunshine,
The stubbornest pangs of resentment
Are cooled to the calm of forgiveness ;
And charity cradles the armor
That was harnessed in bristling anger.

Her mother is summoned with others
At the call of Cortez to assemble,
And Malinche sees mother and brother
Through the soul of an earnest hunger.
She (young in all things but her sorrow,
And with only her nature to prompt her)
Beholds, with the heart of a daughter,
The mother that cruelly spurned her,

In the fading Spring of her lifetime.
The mother, as ready responding
To the tie that her crime would have broken,
Sees her child, like the face of a spectre,
Rising out of the grave to accuse her,
And in terror would fly from her presence ;
But Malinche sprang forward to grasp her,
And, forgetting all else but her mother,
Poured out her full heart in caresses,

Saying, "Surely, my mother, you knew not
When you sold me away to the traders ;
Surely, not with your voice could you sanction,
Your words would have frozen together,
And not with your heart you consented.
The blood would have whited to marble ;
Some artifice surely was practiced.
My mother was *always* my mother ;
And though you unwittingly sold me,
Malinche is free to forgive you.
Take back to your bosom your daughter,
It is all for the best that we parted,
For it gave me my sweet Mary Mother
With her child, the immaculate God-Son;
And better a slave and a Christian,
Than a priest in the pay of the temple.
And, yet, how I longed for a mother,
To show the clear trail for my footsteps,

And to hold the white hand of my childhood !
With no other mother but Mary
(Sweet Mary, the soul of compassion),
I have tried to grow up towards Heaven ;
But a mother on earth is the blessing
That can never be held by another.
Our flesh will not float on the pinions
That bear to Elysian our spirits ;
Our hearts are too warm for the angels,
To hush with their transparent fingers;
Our lips are too ready for kisses
To be cooled to the calm of devotion ;
Our hands are too warm in anothers
To be folded in supplication ;
Too much of the earth is about us
To be lost in the halo of Heaven—
So we need the cool heart of the mother
That has passed the hot chaos of passion,
To temper the pulse that is wayward.

" Yet I cannot have wandered so greatly,
When love was the only impulsion,
Such a distance away from the Master
Whose name is the essence of loving ;
But he sees the bare heart in its throbbing,
And the crystallized faith of my footsteps
That were only too quick in their choosing.
Surely, Love, the benificent Master,

Springing forth from the bosom of Mary,
To smother the earth with caresses,
Will drop a light hand on the shoulder
That shadows a heart that has wandered
By only its warm overflowing."

She loaded her mother with jewels,
And left not the shadow of malice
To stain the fair skirts of her mercy,
But canceled her wrongs with caresses,
And covered the past with forgiveness.
Thus she bore the whole soul of the Gospel
To the hungry hearts of her people;
And the heart is not hard to the sermon
That carries a life for its background
As perfectly pure as the precept.
The heathen is waiting the harvest—
Only hallowed hands for the sickle ;
When the life and the lip move together
Millennium waits on the morning.

The trial that sometimes had shadowed
Comes at last in its fullness upon her,
And the pride of Cortez seeks another
For the place that is only Malinche's.
And he offers to Don Xamarillo
The tremulous hand of the maiden,
As if it was his to bestow her

As a chattel—a token of friendship—
On his friend and bosom companion.
The anger of love was upon her,
And all of her beauty shone brightest,
As she flashed on her recreant lover
The flaming scourge of her protest :

"I came as a slave to your camp-ground;
You lifted me out of my bondage,
For you knew I was free in my birthright.
You wooed me, and won me as lover,
And only as wife could have worn it ;
I have drawn on your love as a garment.
You first sought me out as a sponsor,
But the language of Spain is a magnet
That drew me all out of Malinche
And made me a part of her Chieftain;
And now you would sunder the tendrils
And force back the vine from the branches
Where they learn't all of life in reclining,
And never can unlearn the lesson.

"O, Hernando, you know not Malinche !
If you think she can cherish another
In the heart she too wiilingly gave you ;
Were you priest of the Aztec temple,
And should raise in your hand the itztli,
To open the breast of your victim ;

My heart would leap out at your calling,
E're the word of your summons was spoken.
Ask me to anticipate Heaven,
And my life would be swift in its forfeit.
But to learn the love of another,
And to wean me from your caresses,
Is beyond the wisdom of granting.
The logic of love hath a limit,
Only God can re-tension our heart-strings.

" Oh, Hernando ! my prince and my primate,
My husband on earth and in Heaven !
Let me cling to your feet as a hand-maid,
And wash with my tears, as another
Did moisten the feet of our Savior,
But drive me not hence from your presence.
I can never love Xamarillo—
He can fetter the hand of Malinche,
But her heart will go over the ocean
And will smite at your breast when you proffer
Your hand to some delicate Dona.

" Not alone is the voice of my pleading,
But an angel in Heaven comfronts you ;
The white wings of sweet Catalina,
Shall flutter the breath of your wooing:
You sent her too early to Heaven
To quiet the shade of her anguish.

Two wives—one on earth, one in Heaven—
Throw *their* love and *your* pride in the balance ;
And another whose innocent glances
Should burn all the dross from your nature,
Your child is a witness against you ;
God has sent him a pledge of my wifehood,
To nail the black lie of denying.

" Though no priest gave the mystical signet,
Surely God heard the vows that were spoken
When our hearts took their place at the wedding ;
And who shall say nay to a union,
When Love gives our souls to each other?
God is Love, and no higher can speak it.
O, Hernando ! be father and husband,
Be angel and saint to Malinche !
She kneels, as she would at God's altar,
To plead for the heart you have broken.
O, turn from your pride, and but touch it,
And it will bloom over with blessing,
And will hallow the hand that shall heal it !"

All in vain did she plead with the Chieftain;
His pride was the bane of his footsteps.
The angel of Love would have held him,
But the blood of old Spain was too purple,
And smothered her tender endeavor.
The grip of his purpose still held him,

And Malinche, now passive with anguish,
Was given to Don Xamarillo
With all the sanction of marriage.
He was kind, indulgent and loving,
And she was made wealthy by Cortez
Giving back the estate of her mother
And much of the wealth of the province,
As if he would purchase appeasement.
The Chieftain made lavish atonement,
As far as the world could atone her ;
But her heart was impossible healing.

Though her charities gave her some solace,
And she strove with the earnest of pathos
To lose in the anguish of others
The shadow of self and of sorrow,
Yet she wended her way, broken-hearted ;
And, as if like the spirit of Aztlan,
With the mark of perpetual sadness,
With the head bending over and brooding—
As groping her way to the sunset,
Peering out for the light that was passing
For ever and aye with the shadows—
She fell asleep with her people,
And an angel was born in Heaven.

And a guardian angel descended,
And gathered thy ashes, dead Aztlan !

And spread her white wings o'er the casket,
To wait for the sound of the trumpet
That called thee to life and to freedom.
It rode on the wing of the North Wind,
And shook the whole earth when it sounded.
And no plainer hozanna gave echo,
Than arose from thy halls, Montezuma,
When the shade of Malinche gave battle,
And the armies of Spain were dismembered,
As Mexitli arose from her ashes,
And a star was replanted in Heaven !

And now, in the dusk of the evening,
When lovers await at the casement,
The tokened response of their ladies,
When Chapultepec garlands her tablets
With the beautiful plumage of springtime,
And a thousand sprays of the sunlight
Give her walls all the charm of enchantment,
Malinche is seen through the shadows,
The unsummoned guest at each wedding ;
The unspoken tryst of all lovers;
Wherever two hands are united,
The hand of a third presses o'er them.
The troth of two hearts is cemented
By the one that was cruelly broken.
No symbol of faith can be stronger,
Than " The love that is true as Malinche's."

And she watches the fate of the nation
With the jealous eye of a mother,—
A mother, whose voice more than others
Tought their lips the first lisp of the Gospel,
And tendered their steps toward Heaven.
A saint, at whose shrine they all gather
When the shadow of war hovers o'er them,
And the eagle swoops down from the mountain
To cover the snake with his talons.
And they pledge anew to the banner
That arose again with the nation,
When the three hundred years of their bondage
Forged their broken links into missiles
To drive Spain into the ocean.

Thus she holds the warm palm of her people
With a memory stronger than shadow,—
She lives ; and the Spirit of Aztlan,
"The beautiful sphinx of the ages,"
With its foot at the threshold of empire,
And its hand on the pulse of the sunrise,
And its crown of all possible setting,
Has no brighter gem than Malinche.

———

Blest Mary ! the mother of God,
    And tenderest daughter of Heaven !
Thou, too, hast passed under the rod,

And with thy great sorrow hast striven !
Shall a child of misfortune e'er wait
   On this side the Beautiful City,
 When thy hand is the turn of the gate,
   And thy voice hath the magic of pity ?
No ; the word shall be spoken ere thought,
   And the prayer be granted ere spoken,
And the gate shall swing open unsought
   To the heart that is bleeding and broken.

The devils that tore Magdalene
   May gnash at the sorrow of others;
Since a pitying Christ uttered "peace,"
   Mankind become sisters and brothers.
Our faith hangs not on the morrow,
   But is instant and on the wing ;
With the common signet of sorrow,
   We pass to the court of the King.

THE HARP OF THE WEST.

Fair Clime of the sunset ! more richly endowed
Than Hispan' the knightly, or Gallia the proud—
　　Where the lakes of old Scotia are lost in the maze
Of thy thousand that mirror their heavy fringed banks
Of mountain and crag, and the statliest ranks
　　That ever stood sentinel-watch to the gaze
· Of a sky bending closer, and breathing more near
Than the heart ever throbbed to the fall of a tear.

Though the soul be as barren as Cobi's bleak heath
And the spirit of song in the cold throes of death,
　　Can humanity throttle the play of the breeze
O'er the harp that old Nature unwittingly strung,
When the windows of Heaven wide open were flung,
　　For a thousand years to thy masterful trees ?
Can the ear fail to hear, or the eye fail to see
Thy rich crown ! thy sweet song ! great Yo Semite ?

Though the brow of Olympus be crowded with thrones,
And the cliffs of Parnassus resound with the tones
　　Of the Muses that sang at the foot of their god,
Not Apollo's great steeds, nor the flame of his car,
Nor Mars, with the terrible glitter of war,
　　Can dazzle the face of thy sun and thy sod,

Bright Star of the West ! Thou art Empire's own idol,
The steed of the lightning, untamed to the bridle !

What is History's wreath but a rocord of death !
Time breathes on the tablet, it fades with his breath ;
    But Nature has written in language so strong
That Eternity's finger alone can displace,
And write its own letters to fill up the space.
    Our castles are mountains—our history, long,—
So long that we simply write God on the page,
And leave other Nations to guess at our age.

Our song is the present ; God fills up the past,
With his rock-written letters ; a volume so vast
    No hand may transcribe what He leaves as his own.
From Sinai we came with his prophet of old,
To the valley where glitters the altar of gold—
    Shall we break, in our frenzy, the tables of stone?
No ! the letters are fresh, and deep graven the hand.
Far too sacred our charge ! As He writ, let them stand !

When these tablets of Nature shall yield to the brain,
And some bard shall interpret the words they contain,
    What a song shall burst forth from the prison of
      thought!
As his hand shall pass over the magical strings,
And each chord at his touch into unison springs,
    As the wing of his impulse is hastily caught,
No harp more divine in the turn of the earth
Shall throb to the measures of sorrow and mirth !

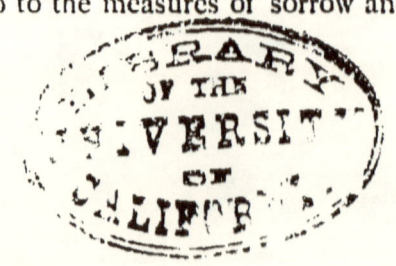